Trusting Cupid

TRACY BROEMMER

Trusting Cupid

by

Tracy Broemmer

Contemporary Romance Novella

Published by Tracy Broemmer

Edited by Lexie Broemmer

Cover by Vanilla Lily Designs

ISBN#: 978-1-951637-66-8

Chapter One

Cupid was decidedly creepy. Olive Cullison had thought so for years, but every year as Valentine's Day came around, she was reminded again of how much she disliked the chubby little god who flung arrows at innocent people to make them fall in love. Had nothing to do with that part, with the *falling in love* part, just the idea of a chubby little boy with a bow and arrow directing things like Captain Stubing from that old 70's TV show, *The Love Boat*.

Eyes on the cardboard Cupid hanging from the ceiling, Olive shuddered. Shouldn't boys that age be outside playing with trucks or even inside watching *The Backyardigans* or something? Not concerning themselves with other people's love lives?

"Aunt Olive!" Lucia tugged on Olive's forearm. Careful not to spill her overpriced but terribly necessary coffee, Olive turned her attention to her niece and eased her arm out of the little girl's grasp.

1

"What, sweetie?"

"Look!!" Lucia reached again for Olive's arm, but Olive dodged her.

"Careful, hon. I don't wanna spill my coffee on you and burn you."

"See? Mr. Harlowe made that for us!"

Olive looked up at the giant mailbox the kindergarten teacher's husband had made for their Valentine's Day party. It was a pretty good replica of the blue boxes on corners all across the country—complete with the words US Postal Service stenciled on it.

"That's really cool, Luce!" Olive followed the little redhead over to the mailbox and crowded in with the rest of the kids and parents gathered there.

"We put our Balentimes in there now, and then when we have our party, the mailman is going to come and deliver them to us."

Olive nodded her approval as she eyed the details of the mailbox. She'd assumed it was made of cardboard, but up close, she could see it was metal. The stenciling was all perfectly straight. Mrs. Harlowe was a lucky woman if her husband was this handy.

"Well, let's do it." Olive glanced at Lucia and arched her eyebrows. "Are you ready?"

Eyes twinkling with excitement, Lucia nodded and dropped her *Paw Patrol* backpack right there on the floor at her feet. Olive's phone buzzed in her hand, but she ignored it for now. Lucia squatted by her bag and tugged the zipper open.

She reached inside to pull out the bundled Valentines Elaina had put together for her.

Leave it to her sister to be so obnoxiously over-the-top. Even nine and a half months pregnant, Elaina had to do all the frills and buttons and bows and whistles for Lucia. Not that Olive didn't think her niece was worth the effort and frills. Nope, simply that Olive didn't have a creative bone in her body.

Lucia handed one bundle up to Olive, who now felt a bit like a circus clown juggling her coffee, her phone, her keys, and the awkward bundle of red envelopes. The top one —*Addler*, it said, in Elaina's giant block print, as neat as if a computer had produced it—had a heart-shaped sucker taped to it. Apparently, they all did, which made the bundle awkward and hard to hold.

Lucia stood again, the other bundle in her hands. She flashed Olive a toothless grin.

"Ready?" Olive smiled at the little girl. Lucia was her only niece, though there would be another baby soon. Like, before the day was over. Elaina and Mark's second baby would be a boy, though, according to their ultrasound. Didn't matter to Olive; she was thrilled to be an aunt again.

"Yes!" Lucia tugged at the ribbon holding her stack together. She stood on her tiptoes and reached for the handle to pull the swing door on the box open. Olive reached to help her when she saw the envelopes in Lucia's little hand start to slide apart. With her pinky finger, she pulled the door open and watched Lucia drop in the cards. She noticed a few names—*Kaeli, Tinsley*, and *Libbie*—as the envelopes dropped into the mailbox. When Lucia's hands were empty, Olive let the door close and tried to hand the little girl the second stack.

"You do it!" Lucia clapped her hands together, apparently thrilled with the experience. So much so, she didn't want Olive to miss out on the fun.

"You do it, sweetie," Olive insisted. "They're your Valentines for your classmates."

One of said classmates bumped into Lucia and knocked her into Olive's legs. Lucia shook her head and stared up at Olive with wide, green eyes.

"What?" Olive shifted on her feet and attempted to pat Lucia on the shoulder to comfort her. Hands full, she squatted down to Lucia's level instead.

"Those are the boys' cards." Lucia leaned close and whispered the words, her warm breath tickling Olive's ear.

"That's okay—"

Lucia cut her off with a severe head shake. This time when she leaned closer, she nearly knocked Olive over.

"There's one for Braden," she whispered.

"Braden?" Olive repeated quietly, eyes locked with her niece's. Lucia only nodded. "Is he your boyfriend?"

"No!" Lucia looked stricken by the thought. "Will you do it? Please?"

Worried now that her niece would get upset over someone named Braden, maybe remember that her mommy was in the hospital today to have a baby, and end up having a meltdown, Olive nodded.

"Of course I will, sweetie."

Olive straightened, but she took one more look at Lucia before tossing the cards into the box.

"You're sure?"

Lucia, face still frozen with worry, answered with a quick nod.

Olive tugged the swing door down with her pinky again, still cradling her coffee with her remaining fingers and thumb, and pushed the envelopes into the slot just as someone bumped into her from behind. The envelopes hit the bottom with a loud clang. Olive pulled her hand away, lifted her coffee for a sip, and winked at Lucia.

"I'm so sorry." The sincere deep voice behind her told her the perpetrator who bumped into her was a parent—a dad —and not a kid. "Are you okay?"

"All done!" She lifted her hand, palm up, as if to say no big deal. And realized she'd dropped her phone and her keys into the mailbox along with Lucia's cards.

Chapter Two

KIRBY

"Oh no!"

Kirby Owens blinked at the look of horror on the woman's face. Had he hurt her? He didn't think he'd bumped into her that hard, but that little terror child had nailed him in the back, so maybe he'd knocked the woman into the mailbox? It wasn't cardboard, so that might hurt, he guessed.

"Are you okay?" He reached for her with both hands, fingers barely brushing her forearms.

"My phone." She nodded, eyes locked with his. "My phone and my keys."

Kirby tipped his chin to his chest and swept the floor of the classroom with his gaze. A crayon the color of macaroni and cheese. A Spiderman sticker that appeared to be stuck to the floor. And Libbie Godfrey's lunchbox.

No phone or keys.

"Did you drop them?" he asked when he finally looked back at her.

She nodded again, eyes wide with horror.

"In the mailbox," she whispered.

"Oh." His response might have been a bit exaggerated, but her panic was so real, he felt it, too.

"Aunt Olive, what's the matter?"

Kirby jerked his gaze to the little redhead tugging at the woman's arm now. Olive, he assumed, was quick to pass her coffee cup to her other hand so it wouldn't spill.

"I dropped my keys and my phone, hon."

"I'll get them." The little girl shrugged and squatted with ease to look around on the floor. Kirby watched with amusement as the little girl picked up the crayon with a sigh, tried for a second to peel the sticker from the floor, and then slipped onto her knees to crawl around in search of the missing phone and keys.

"Lucia, I dropped them in the mailbox," the woman told the girl. Kirby watched her whip her head around in a desperate search for a place to set her coffee cup. Wanting to help, since he felt responsible, Kirby held out his hand. The woman named Olive paused just long enough to flash a grateful smile and hand him the cup.

He watched as she leaned over and snatched the little redhead off the floor.

"You're gonna get your leggings dirty, sweetie."

"But your phone—"

"I'll take care of it," Olive promised her.

"What if Daddy tries to call—"

"I'll just ask Mrs. Harlowe to get it for me."

"She said we can't open the mailbox until it's time for the party!" Lucia shook her head, clearly as upset with the phone situation as the woman.

"I'm sure she can open it just to grab my phone and keys." The woman sounded calm enough that the little girl seemed to settle down. But Henry chose that moment to jump into the conversation. Leaning hard into Kirby's legs, he looped his arm around them and shook his head.

"Nope. Mrs. Harlowe said *no way, Jose*, can it be opened until Mr. Harlowe comes in this afternoon to be the mailman."

The woman peeked at Henry and then looked back at Kirby. Before she could open her mouth again, the bell rang. Kirby dropped his free hand to Henry's head and tousled his hair as the woman took her cup back from him.

"You better get to your seat." He looked down just as Henry looked up at him with a nod. "I'll see you for the big party, okay?"

"Bye, Dad." Henry nodded, but he didn't immediately go to his seat. Instead, he took the little redhead by the hand and tugged gently. "C'mon, Lucia."

"But—"

"It's okay, Luce." The woman squatted again to look the little girl in the eyes. "I'll get it figured out. You don't need to worry about it."

8

"But what about Mommy—"

"Promise." Olive shook her head. "I'll take care of it. And I'll check on Mommy as soon as I leave here."

The little girl stared at the woman for a long moment before finally giving in with a nod. Kirby watched her throw her arms around the woman's neck, squeeze, and finally turn and hurry away with Henry. Rather than sit down, Henry walked her to the cubbies and waited while she hung up her backpack.

"Hmm."

Kirby turned back to look at the woman, but she was watching the kids with a hint of a smile on her face. She jerked her gaze away from them as they headed to their seats and looked at Kirby.

"Guess I need to talk to Mrs. Harlowe."

Still feeling responsible for her losing her keys and phone, Kirby waggled his brows and followed her toward the front of the classroom where Mrs. Harlowe rested her bottom on the edge of the desk.

"Hi, Mrs. Harlowe." The woman's tone suggested she was experienced in talking with unreasonable individuals. Kirby wondered if that meant kids or if she worked with people like that. "I'm Lucia Franklin's aunt. Olive Cullison."

"Hi." Mrs. Harlowe was an older teacher, the grandma type. Henry liked her—she was fair and fun. However, Henry had mentioned more than once that she was very strict and did not bend the rules.

Ever.

"I was helping Luce put her Valentines in the box and dropped my phone and keys inside. Is there any way you can help me—"

"Oh, I'm afraid not." The woman wore an apologetic look on her face, but she shook her head no. "My husband has the key to the mailbox, and he's at work. He'll be in later for the party, though—"

"Mrs. Harlowe." Kirby stepped around Olive. "Hi, I'm Kirby —Henry's dad. Listen, I feel terrible about this. I bumped into Ms. Cullison and made her drop her things. Surely, there's something—"

Mrs. Harlowe cut him off with a head shake.

"I told the kids this when we put the mailbox in here. It's locked. There's no changing our minds and getting anything back out. We're all sending everyone a Valentine. So, the box is locked until Howard gets here with the key."

"Could you maybe call Howard?"

"He's in transit right now," Mrs. Harlowe explained. "Driving a car up to Springfield for the Buick dealership."

Olive Cullison sighed.

"My sister is in the hospital right now. They've probably already induced her."

"I'm sorry."

Kirby got the feeling from the way the teacher lifted her eyes to look over Olive's shoulder that she wasn't all that sorry or even interested in her situation.

"Come back around two thirty," she said with a quick glance at Olive. "We'll be having punch and cookies, and we'll get your things then."

Olive stared after her, clearly shocked, as the teacher stepped away from the desk and raised her voice to address the children. She glanced at Kirby, her pretty face arranged in a frown.

"Did that really just happen?" she whispered.

"It did," he answered with a nod. "And I feel horrible about this."

"Oh, please." She shook her head. "It's not your fault."

"C'mon." Kirby nodded to the door, relieved when she followed him out to the hall. "Listen. Can I drive you somewhere? To the hospital, maybe? Your sister's having a baby, you said?"

Olive sighed and pinched the bridge of her freckled nose.

"Yeah. She's, like, three years overdue, and on the day they induce her, I pull a classic move and lose my phone and keys."

She shot him a grin and rolled her eyes.

"Three years overdue, huh?" Kirby arched his eyebrows. "I think I feel sorry for her husband."

Olive snorted.

"C'mon. A ride is the least I can do."

Chapter Three

OLIVE

"I still can't believe I did that." Olive dropped her head back and stared at the ceiling in the hall for a second before following the guy outside.

"Well, if I hadn't waylaid you—"

"You didn't waylay me. I was juggling too much stuff—"

"Yeah, but if that Braden hadn't nailed me in the back—"

Olive stopped walking and tipped her head at the guy when he glanced back at her.

"Oh. I'm the black Subaru over at the end of the parking lot."

"Braden." Olive started walking again. Wasn't that the name Lucia had whispered to her? Her niece hadn't wanted to drop the boys' cards into the mailbox because Braden's was in there.

"Oh yeah." The guy nodded as he walked. "Braden. Gosh, that kid's bound to be a mob enforcer when he gets older. He looks like a fifth grader."

Olive snorted. The guy stopped at the black Subaru and pulled the passenger door open for her.

"Oh." He offered her a slow grin. Olive took a moment to study him—unruly blond hair, bright blue eyes, and a long, slender nose that fit his thin angular face just right. "I'm Kirby Owens. Henry's dad."

"Nice to meet you, Kirby. I'm Olive Cullison. I'm Lucia's aunt."

"And her mom's havin' a baby today." Kirby nodded.

"My sister," Olive answered. "I wanna know more about this Braden kid."

Kirby nodded for her to get in and then closed the door when she did. The interior of the car wasn't immaculate, but it was clean. A half empty bottle of water sat in the cup holder. Two quarters and a nickel were on the console. There was a fine layer of dust on the dashboard, but then there was a fine layer of dust on every surface in Olive's life on a regular basis.

"Hey. Do you wanna get some coffee—" Kirby slid into his seat and then glanced at her and stopped, reminded that she already had coffee.

"Actually, I would love another cup of hot coffee," Olive confessed. "I'm not used to this kid routine. I'm exhausted already."

"What about the hospital?"

Olive set her cup in the other cup holder and reached for her seatbelt. She needed to check in, but she also doubted Elaina was in active labor yet. Not that she knew anything about having babies. But it had taken Elaina twelve hours with Lucia. And Olive had heard countless horror stories from girlfriends who had given birth.

"Um." She tipped her head and arched her eyebrows. "Could I borrow your phone?"

"Yeah, of course." He nodded and pulled it from his coat pocket. "You could give them my number in case they need to reach you."

"Are you sure you don't mind?"

"Of course I don't mind," he answered as he started the car.

Kirby backed out of his space and eased the car out of the parking lot as Olive dialed her brother-in-law's number. Mark answered on the third ring, still sounding excited and chipper. Olive knew from the long ordeal of Lucia's birth that his energy would wane just as Elaina's did.

"Hello?"

"Mark, it's Olive."

"Olive? Whose phone is this?"

"I dropped mine. Listen, can you just call me on this number—"

"Dropped it?" Mark interrupted her. "Did it shatter?"

Olive heard her sister's voice in the background. She sounded upbeat, too. Relief eased the tension in her shoulders and neck. Their mother was half a world away; she would lecture Olive six ways from Sunday if she knew she'd lost her phone at such a crucial time. Olive was her stand-in —support for Mark, someone to watch Lucia, and someone to swoop in and care for the baby so Elaina and Mark could rest. Not that she minded. But she didn't need the extra worry about being unavailable when Mark called.

"Mark, just call me on this number—"

"Does she have a burner phone?"

Olive felt Kirby's eyes on her. She rolled her eyes at her sister's question.

"Please? Just keep this number for a while. If you need me, call me on this number?"

"Got it," Mark agreed. "She's doing fine, by the way. Kind of cranky."

Olive figured that earned him a swat if he was anywhere within Elaina's reach.

"Thanks." Olive ended the call and set Kirby's phone on the console.

"Everything okay?"

"Yeah. Sounds like it."

"Is it just the two of you?"

Olive watched the dirty slushy snow on the street as Kirby drove. She nodded and then spoke out loud since he was hopefully watching the road.

"Yeah. Just the two of us. And my mom's doing a European river cruise right now, so I'm it."

"You ever done one of those?"

"A European river cruise?" Olive glanced at him and shook her head when he nodded. "No. I've done a few Caribbean cruises."

"Hey. We could get coffee at the new little bakery just a couple blocks from the hospital."

Olive shrugged. She'd grown up here, but she had moved away after college. Things had changed quite a bit since then.

"Sure. Sounds good."

"So, you don't know Braden, then."

"No." Olive laughed when he looked at her again and their eyes met. "I mean, I'm in town a lot, I guess. But we just spend most of our time at Elaina's house. And I talk to Lucia all the time, but I've never heard her talk about Braden. Mostly Libbie and Kaeli."

"Where are you from?" Kirby drove down Broadway with ease, left hand slung over the top of the steering wheel and his right resting on his leg. Olive liked how comfortable he seemed—even with a strange mad woman who had dropped her phone and keys in a mailbox on his hands. He wasn't a big guy, but he was tall and lanky. His seat was back a bit to give him some leg space.

"I grew up here." She looked around as he drove west. "But I went away for college and never came back."

"Where'd you go to school?"

"Illinois State." She watched a McDonald's go by and felt a pang of sadness that the place now looked more like a depressing office building than a fun fast food and play place for kids. "I stayed in Normal after school."

The only sound for a few moments was the radio. Olive recognized the seventies song playing and mentally approved. Kirby Owens was an interesting man.

"What about you?" she asked him when the song ended and a commercial for car insurance started.

"Grew up in southern Missouri." He flipped his turn signal on and eased into the right turn lane. Olive saw a cute little gray-sided building on the approaching corner and decided it must be the new place Kirby had mentioned. "And I went to Mizzou."

She wondered what brought him here. Maybe his wife.

She also wondered where his wife was and what she would think about this little coffee date. Not that it was a *date* date. But still.

Kirby turned into the corner lot and pulled into a spot next to a Toyota Forerunner. Olive grabbed her cup to throw it away when she got out and jammed her other hand into her coat pocket. She found it interesting that February was the shortest month of winter, but to her, it often seemed to drag on forever. Maybe just because she tended to get the winter blues, and by this time every year, she was desperate for sunshine and warmer temperatures.

Cardboard cupids and pink hearts hung on strings inside the coffee place. Olive gave Kirby an eye roll when they stepped inside, but they shared a quick laugh.

"But their donuts are *so* good," he told her as they stepped up to the counter.

17

"Sweethearts' special," the older woman at the counter chirped with a smile. "Two pastries and two coffees for the price of one."

"Oh, we're not—" Olive started.

"Perfect." Kirby drummed his fingers on the counter and studied the donuts behind the glass. "What would you like, Olive?"

Chapter Four

KIRBY

Kirby chewed the last bite of his bear claw as Olive plucked another tiny bite of her cream-filled donut and slipped it in her mouth.

"So, tell me about Braden the mob enforcer." She met his eyes as she swallowed.

He laughed and shrugged. "You think I'm kidding, but Henry says the kid's just mean."

"Does he get in trouble?"

"Yeah, he does, but it doesn't seem to bother him."

"Lucia didn't want to put the boys' cards in the box today, because Braden's was in the stack. That's why I did it."

"Henry says he pulls the girls' hair all the time."

"Great." Olive rolled her eyes and picked at her donut again. "He'll probably be one of those boys who snaps bra straps in fifth grade and drugs girls in high school."

Kirby flinched.

"Sorry." Olive laughed and covered her face with her hand. "I get a little protective of my niece. That was probably too far."

"I'm thinking he might skip the drugs and use brutal force," Kirby admitted. "Henry saw him knock down a second grader on the playground this year."

"Oh no." Olive dropped her hand to her lap. "Does he pick on Henry?"

"Tried at the beginning of the year. Henry fought back."

"He did? Your little guy fought back?"

"Yeah." Kirby nodded. "They both got in trouble that day, but at least the enforcer leaves Henry alone now."

Olive sipped her coffee and lowered her eyes to his phone, screen up on the table.

"What would your wife think of you babysitting some ditz who tossed her phone and keys in a mailbox?"

"You're hardly a ditz," he argued with a grin. "Besides, you had help."

"I shouldn't have had my hands so full."

Kirby shrugged. "I lost my wife when Henry was two."

Olive froze, coffee cup halfway between her mouth and the table.

Kirby flinched; he hated the way people treated him when he told them he was a widower. Yes, Jill was the love of his life, and yes, he and Henry lost her way too soon. But he still felt blessed to have his son—not just because he was part of the woman he loved, but because Henry was a bright little boy with a future as big as the sky, and Kirby was ready to see what his son would do with the world.

"Car accident," he said quietly. "She was driving on a two-lane highway and slid on ice into the oncoming lane. Truck hit her head on."

"Oh my God, Kirby." Pale now, Olive set her cup down and pressed her lips together. "I'm sorry."

He nodded. "She was with two girlfriends. They'd been at a convention. All three of them died on scene."

"I lost my dad in a boating accident." She spoke softly, eyes on the table now. "He was only fifty-six when it happened. It's...I can't imagine how difficult that was for you. Especially with having a toddler at home."

Kirby nodded, but he shrugged at the same time. "Henry gives me something to live for."

"I understand." She lifted her eyes to look at him and offered him a quick smile.

"Do you not like the donut?"

Olive glanced at his empty saucer plate and tipped her head back to roar with laughter. The sound was a balm on the exposed side of his heart. Not to mention, that rush of color in Olive's cheeks made her even prettier.

"I love the donut," she answered. "I'm so sorry. I'm keeping you from work. From a girlfriend. From something—"

"You're not," he insisted. "Really, you're not. I just feel like I must've inhaled mine."

"I'm trying *not* to inhale mine," she confessed. Now her cheeks were tinged with pink, like she was embarrassed. "I love marshmallow crème donuts. I could have wolfed down two or three by now. Gotta be careful."

"I'm happy to grab another one for you."

"Please. I had to dance to get these jeans on as it is."

Kirby had seen her in the classroom before he bumped into her. Dark wash jeans and chunky gray ankle boots. The wool pea coat covered her top half, but it stopped at her waist, giving him a nice view of the fit of denim on her bottom. He liked the way the jeans fit, and if he was going to be honest with himself, he liked the idea of her dancing to shimmy into the skinny fit. He wouldn't have minded watching her moves.

"You wear them well," he told her.

There was that little pink flush again. He didn't date much, and he spent most of his time with Henry. But he watched TV and movies, and it kind of surprised him that there were still women who actually blushed when complimented. Seemed like the whole world had gone a little over-the-top crazy with all the social niceties and expectations. In fact, maybe he shouldn't have commented on her jeans at all.

Still smiling, Olive picked up the remainder of the donut and nibbled on it. Kirby held his breath when she glanced at him—a spot of the marshmallow cream on her lips.

"What do you do?" she asked as she flicked her tongue out and licked the cream.

He *didn't* date much, and he couldn't remember the last time he'd had sex, the last time he'd even been attracted to anyone other than Jill. Apparently, it had been a very long time if he was getting hard just watching a pretty woman enjoy a donut.

He stirred from his thoughts—fantasies?—when she put the donut down and reached for her napkin.

"Um." He gave himself a mental shake and then tore his gaze away from her face, from her mouth. "I'm a writer."

"Like a sportswriter?" she asked, obviously unaware of the completely inappropriate thoughts exploding in his brain. He wasn't the kind of guy to objectify women. Even after losing Jill, he didn't tuck his little boy in at night and surf the web looking for porn to take the edge off.

But right now, he couldn't shake the image of the woman across the table from him flicking her tongue over her lips. Maybe over his lips. Down his neck.

"Do you write for the paper?"

"No." He cleared his throat. "No. I write children's books."

"You what?"

"Yeah." He shrugged. "I like baseball as much as the next guy, but I write children's books."

"You write children's books," she repeated. Dammit all. Now she leaned closer, propped her elbow on the table, and rested her chin in her hand. She stared at him intensely and sank her perfect white teeth into her bottom lip.

The same one she just licked the cream from.

"Anything I've heard of?"

"The *Bones Malone* series."

"The *Bones*—? You write the *Bones Malone* series?"

Kirby nodded.

"Wait." She sat back and patted her pockets and then reached for her coat.

"What're you doing?"

"Looking for my—" She groaned and rested against her chair. "I was gonna look up the latest in the series. Lucia loves those books."

Kirby picked up his phone and tapped the screen, aware of her eyes on him. What did she see? Not a seductress with pretty eyes, thick dark curls, and a mouth that looked like it knew how to sin. Nope. She probably saw a dork dad in plain jeans and a flannel shirt over a Rocky and Bullwinkle t-shirt, who dabbled and doodled in kids' stuff on a daily basis.

Guys like him didn't manage to win the pretty girls once in a lifetime. He'd done it with Jill, though honestly, he still didn't always know what she'd seen in him. No way he would get lucky enough to win the interest of another pretty woman.

Their fingers brushed when he handed the phone to her over the table. She looked at him then but only briefly, and then she was gaping at the phone screen, where he'd pulled up the latest Bones Malone picture book on Amazon.

Bones Malone and the Case of the Missing Biscuit. MK Owens.

"That's..." She shrugged. When she tipped her head up again, she wore an excited grin. "I'm speechless. These books are great."

"Thank you."

"Do you do the illustrations, too?"

He nodded. "Jill used to do some of them. But I've done all the Bones Malone pictures."

"Do the kids at school know?"

"No. Well." He flinched and wavered. "Sort of? Henry told one of the boys, and Braden overheard him. When the school year first started."

"Oh." Olive cringed. "And that's when Braden..."

"Yeah. Braden called him a liar. Henry argued. They did some pushing."

"Does Mrs. Harlowe know?"

"She does." Kirby squirmed a bit under her heavy stare. "I'll be reading to the class one of these days. She asked me about it a few months ago."

"Wow." Olive nibbled on her lip again. "That's so cool."

She handed the phone back to him just as it buzzed in her hand.

"Is that your brother-in-law's number?"

Chapter Five

Kirby

"Yes."

Kirby handed his phone back over the table, noticing she was careful not to touch his fingers this time when she took it. Did that mean something? Did it mean she'd felt that little jolt of awareness earlier? The one he did? Or maybe that she hadn't felt anything and didn't want to repeat the awkwardness?

He watched her tip her head and tap the screen before putting his phone to her ear, but when she spoke, he averted his eyes to give her some semblance of privacy. Obviously, he could hear her, but he tried to tune her out.

He could be at home working, but he didn't mind being here with her. In fact, it felt kind of good to be out of his home office, talking to someone. Not just someone—a pretty, vibrant woman. Whether she felt any attraction or not, she was funny and easy to talk to, so no, he didn't mind taking a day off from his self-imposed grueling schedule.

Eyes on the street behind her, he heard her thank her brother-in-law for calling and then say goodbye. She handed his phone back to him with a sheepish smile.

"I'm sorry." She shook her head. The little trill of laughter touched Kirby. He hadn't realized how much he missed having a woman in his life. And no, he wasn't delusional. He didn't think anything would come of spending the day with Lucia Franklin's aunt. But since losing Jill, he hadn't realized how much he missed just the simple things— conversation and yes, laughter.

"Please." He rolled his eyes. "It's fine."

"It feels weird to answer your phone." Olive picked up her coffee again for a drink.

"Is your sister okay?"

"Mmm." She nodded enthusiastically. "Okay, but no progress yet."

"Is your brother-in-law okay?" Kirby tipped his head and narrowed his eyes at her, a little bit thrilled when Olive rewarded him with a little snort of laughter.

"So far, yes."

"Do they know what they're having?"

"A boy."

"So, they'll have the best of both worlds."

"They will."

Kirby dragged his gaze away from her intense stare. He and Jill had wanted more children, but it wasn't meant to be. Kirby supposed Henry would be fine growing up as an only child. Even as an only child without his mother, because Kirby was a hands-on dad. But it did sadden him, the way life had turned out for him, for them.

"Did you want more? Kids?"

Kirby flicked his gaze back to her, drawn to her warm eyes.

"God, I'm sorry." She groaned and shook her head. "Totally none of my business."

"We did want more," he answered without arguing whether it was her business or not. Something about Olive Cullison made him want to talk. In fact, he would be happy to sit here all day and talk to her.

Olive winced as if she felt bad for dredging up the past for him.

"Not the same thing by any means," she began quietly. "I was engaged. Just a few years out of college. We had most of the wedding planned. Most of our lives planned, really." Here, she looked away, flicked her eyes back over Kirby, and looked away again. "He was a financial advisor. About three months before the wedding, he was arrested for embezzling money from one of his client corporations."

Kirby watched her face for a moment, searching for signs of heartache. What he saw was more of an old, residual sadness. Probably much the same as what he wore when he thought of Jill.

"Oh, Olive."

She whipped her eyes back up to his face when he spoke.

"I'm sorry."

"Better that it happened when it did and not after we were married. Imagine if we'd had kids." She squirmed a bit in her chair. "I didn't mean to compare my loss to yours. I just can't imagine how badly it would hurt to lose someone you love so much. Someone you've shared so much life with."

"So, you dumped the guy?" Kirby arched his eyebrows. "Right?"

"I did." She nodded. "Maybe I should have stuck with him, but I couldn't trust a man who's dishonest in his professional life to be honest in his personal life. Not to mention, he went to prison. I needed a clean break."

"Well, of course you did," Kirby agreed. "Tell me you've moved on from that disaster."

She laughed softly. "I've dated. Some."

"No one waiting for you to get back to Normal?"

They shared a laugh at Kirby's unintended pun.

"No."

"Are you afraid? To trust?"

Olive huffed out a long sigh. "I was at first." She shrugged. "But no? Not anymore. I just haven't fallen for anyone. Does that make sense? I have a lot of guy friends. I have friends who try to set me up. But I just haven't felt the way I think I'm supposed to feel for anyone to get serious."

"How do you think it feels? Falling for someone?"

"Like falling," she answered simply. "Like you light up in that person's presence, because being together makes you even more of who you are. And you like who you are when you're with that person. And you're just caught in a free fall."

When she stopped talking, she met his eyes and snorted. "Or maybe, all of this Cupid crap is going to my brain."

"Cupid crap, huh?"

"Not a believer." She shook her head.

"Well, I mean." Kirby tipped his head back and gestured at a Cupid cutout hanging directly over their table. "Look. He's this short, fat little cherub thing that looks like Henry as a baby. I used to change those diapers. I don't get why anyone would think it's a good idea to put love arrows in a baby's hand and ask him to make some love matches."

Olive laughed so loud, she clapped her hand over her mouth.

"I mean, Henry was still drooling and wearing more food than I could get in his mouth at that stage. Cute little dude, but c'mon."

"Cupid's not cute, though," Olive argued. "He's creepy."

"Oh, I agree. Totally." Kirby nodded.

"Then again, online dating sucks, too, so. Who knows?"

Kirby cringed. "Oh man. You've done the swipe right thing, huh?"

"For a brief time." She nodded. "I plead temporary insanity."

"No perfect matches, huh?"

"My girlfriends talked me into it," she explained. "I did two dates. Two different guys. The first one wanted me to come home with him and meet his mom that first night. After a breakfast for dinner date at a local diner. Don't get me wrong. Good food. But the guy spent the whole date talking about his dog when he was seven. Except for when he told me about his brother and how they used to go fishing and clean their catches."

"Nice."

"Right?" Olive laughed.

"And the other one?"

She flinched. Kirby noticed the flush in her cheeks again.

"We had dinner at an Italian place. Very fancy. He talked nonstop about his job. Which changed twice over dinner. First, he was a doctor, and then he was talking about being in a courtroom. He got angry when I called him out on it."

"So, the date ended early."

"Sort of?" She frowned and shook her head. "He still drove me home. And he still kissed me goodnight. And it was pretty horrible."

"I hope you don't let that stop you from ever kissing anyone again."

Olive's little smile twisted his heart into knots.

"That *was* my last kiss, actually," she said softly. "Yeah, maybe I need to just grab someone and lay one on him to wipe out that bad memory."

Their eyes met again. Kirby was proud of himself for not offering to help her clear her memory.

"Do you want more coffee?" he asked her. She probably didn't. Not after having some earlier when they'd bumped into each other and having more now. God knows, Kirby didn't need more. His heart was thumping so rapidly right now, so loud, he figured Olive could hear it. Maybe she could see it pounding right out of his chest and moving his shirt.

More coffee might send him into a stroke.

But he had to put some distance between them and the talk about kissing.

Chapter Six

OLIVE

"No." She rolled her eyes. "I don't think I need more coffee. Should we get out of here?"

"Yeah." Kirby looked up again, eyes sweeping the whole place and all the Cupids and hearts hanging from the ceiling. "Maybe we should before one of us gets hit with an arrow."

Olive laughed again and gathered up her napkins.

"Do you want me to take you to the hospital?"

She hesitated but finally nodded. "Yeah. I just wish I had known when I left Elaina's house this morning that I was going to do something so dumb. I could have brought my computer or a book or something." She glanced at him as they stood. "Then again, I guess anything I'd have brought with me would be locked in my car right now."

Kirby nodded. "True."

"I'll make Mark buy me a book at the hospital gift shop." She shrugged as she tossed her trash into the receptacle and stepped aside.

"Or." Kirby shrugged and disposed of his own napkins and cup. "What about a sneak peek at the next Bones Malone book?"

Olive looked up at him as they walked out of the coffee shop side by side.

"Really?"

He glanced at her with a smile. "Well, I mean, I can take you to the hospital. If that's what you want. But I was thinking maybe you could be my date for a pretty happening Valentine's party this afternoon. So, we could hang out for a while."

"But you would show me a sneak peek?"

"Sure." Kirby nodded. "Is your sister expecting you at the hospital?"

"No." Olive watched Kirby step in front of her as they crossed the parking lot so he could open her door for her again. He was kind of old-fashioned, but she liked that about him. She liked a lot about him, and that was a little bit dangerous. Olive was never above making new friends, but it wouldn't do any good to like this guy for anything more than that. Not when he lived here, and her life was four hours away.

"I was with her when Lucia was born," Olive told him as she slid into the passenger seat. She watched him move around the front of the SUV, noticing the snug way his jeans fit his hips. Not tight. Nothing flashy. But a good, solid fit.

"Too much for you, huh?" he asked when he dropped into the driver's seat.

"It was fascinating," she said absently. "But, yeah, kind of made me a little squeamish."

"You don't do blood?"

"I'm not sure I could squeeze a wailing infant out my—" She stopped talking and looked away with a laugh. "What is it about you? You're so easy to talk to."

"Yeah, well, kudos to all women who give birth," Kirby agreed with a nod in her direction. "Incredible to witness. And I don't blame you for feeling a little nervous about it."

Olive nibbled on her lip and told herself not to say what she was thinking.

"The first time I had sex hurt like hell," she mumbled, cheeks flaring with embarrassment. "At the time I couldn't imagine anything bigger inside me. Not to mention trying to push a small human out of me."

Kirby snorted.

"You spiked the coffee. Didn't you?" She glanced at him, embarrassed. But they shared a look of disbelief and then both laughed.

"I kind of wish I had," he answered. "What would you say to me if you had a shot of truth juice in your coffee?"

"I'm sorry." She shook her head and dipped her chin to hide her face.

"Don't be."

From the corner of her eye, she saw him shrug. "It's a natural part of life, right? A woman's body is made to do that. I think it's incredible. And scary as hell, yes."

Relief flooded her when he turned the radio up a smidge before pulling out of his parking spot. She relaxed back into her seat, happy to cruise along with The Commodores serenading her.

"How old were you?"

"Eighteen."

"Did you ever find anything bigger?"

Olive laughed and closed her eyes. "Yeah. I did. And it's all good."

Kirby turned and grinned at her when she peeked at him.

"Jill had a panic attack when she was about seven months along with Henry. Thinking about the end process. She was thrilled when she found out she was pregnant. We both were. And we couldn't wait to do the parent thing, ya know? But then, one night, it just hit her—what she would have to do to have that baby, for us to really be parents."

"Yeah?" Olive turned her head to watch him, curious if all women felt that same mix of fear and excitement. Her friends had mentioned nerves about the birthing process, but once they had their babies, they were all full of smug wisdom, promising her she would forget the pain and it was all worth it when she had her baby in her arms.

Maybe so. But being that she hadn't even been pregnant, she was still hung up on the big event.

"Yeah. She ate a whole package of licorice that night."

"Ooh."

"Black licorice."

"Even worse."

"Right?" He nodded and looked her way again. "I hate black licorice."

"Me too." Olive nodded. "Did it help her settle down?"

"No." Kirby grinned. "I gave her a foot rub, and we ended up having sex."

"See? Now that's another thing I worry about."

"Having sex when you're pregnant?" He shrugged. "It doesn't hurt the baby."

"No, but how is it sexy?" Olive shook her head. "How is it even done?"

Kirby glanced at her again, and this time, Olive gave herself a mental shake. "Don't answer that. How did we get on this topic? Tell me about Bones Malone's next adventure."

"I'm going to show you," he reminded her. "Are you asking me how I found my seven-month pregnant wife sexy?"

"I'm asking you nothing of the sort." She crossed her heart with her solemn vow. "Please strike the whole conversation from the record."

"Done." He nodded.

"Thank you."

"What do you do?" he asked her after a few moments had passed. Despite the absurd rabbit hole of conversation they'd gone down, Olive was relaxed and comfortable, watching the businesses and store fronts pass by as Kirby drove.

"I'm an accountant," she answered. "CPA. But right now, I'm doing bookkeeping for a trucking company. I'm lucky enough I can work from home—or Elaina's house—if I need to."

"You don't strike me as a numbers kind of person."

"No?" She looked back at him. "How do I strike you?"

"You're too adventurous and fun to crunch numbers for a living."

"I think that might be the first time anyone's called me adventurous or fun. That's my sister, actually."

"Nope." Kirby shook his head. "It's you."

"What would you have guessed I did?"

"Ummmm." He pursed his lips as he considered her question. "Something creative. Like...graphic design or marketing."

"Really?"

"Yeah. I think you'd be really good at it."

Olive stared at him silently for a moment, oddly pleased with his observations. She liked her job. And she loved her sister. But she'd always been content to stand in Elaina's shadow and let her be the spontaneous, fun sister.

"My dad always told me I was the grounded daughter. The logical one. I don't think he meant to judge either of us. He just saw Laine as being spirited and hyper. And I was the quiet, logical one."

Olive mulled that over for a few moments.

"Elaina studied marketing in school. And she did some graphic design."

Kirby eyed her curiously for a moment. "And now?"

"She owns an interior design business. She's got the eye for it."

Kirby looked back at the windshield, leaving Olive alone in her thoughts again.

"Where do you live?" she asked when he made a right turn on Sixteenth Street.

"In a giant, old house on Connecticut."

Olive had been gone for a while, but she knew he was talking about the historic district.

"Nice."

"Jill was hoping it was haunted when we moved in. No such luck."

Chapter Seven

KIRBY

Kirby tried to see the skinny two-story brick home through Olive's eyes as he pulled the Subaru into the long, narrow driveway. The house was a mix of old and new; he'd fixed up some things, replaced some windows and gutters, painted a few rooms. None of it was in total disrepair, but there were still rooms he wanted to paint, flooring he wanted to redo.

Still, he loved the place. He and Jill had lived here for a year before she got pregnant. They'd tackled the kitchen remodel together, enjoying the hard work, the feeling of accomplishment that came with the new, updated room, and just the time spent together. Now that it was just him and Henry, Kirby still loved the house. It was home. The upstairs was a bit drafty, but blankets and space heaters and love made it a cozy home for him and his little boy.

With a shake of his head, Kirby killed the engine and got out. He could park in the garage. Used to be that Jill's car went in the garage. Now, unfortunately, it was all his. But there was no precipitation in the forecast, and no matter if he took Olive to the hospital or back to the school for the party, he would have to leave again at some point.

Olive was right. She'd said there was something about him that made him easy to talk to. So much so she'd rattled on about sex and having babies, to the point she was embarrassed. For the record, Kirby was torn between thinking she was cute and being a little bit turned on—the mention of her first time having sex did it—and he didn't want her to be embarrassed about it. But there was something about *Olive* that made *Kirby* want to talk. Made him want to share more of his life, of his and Henry's life with her.

Obviously. He was about to welcome her into their home.

"I love this neighborhood." Olive's announcement was laced with wonder. She walked at his side to the front porch, but her head was tipped back, and she was looking up at the house. And the neighboring houses. "I had a friend who lived a few blocks over. I loved going to her house."

"I like it," he agreed with her. "It's a good place for Henry. There are a few kids around his age on the block, but it's quiet, too."

"What does Henry like to do?"

Kirby unlocked the door and opened it to usher her inside.

"He's into superheroes. And basketball."

"Who's his favorite?"

"The Bulls," Kirby answered with a grin. Olive rolled her eyes at him. He fished around in the mailbox outside the door before stepping inside.

"I meant—"

"I know what you meant." He nodded. "Spiderman, of course."

"Luce likes the Hulk."

"And you?"

"Ironman."

"Not Thor?"

"Nah." Olive shook her head. "I mean, he's nice to look at. But."

Kirby grinned and closed the door.

"Okay. So, let's go see what Bones is up to."

"Where did you get the idea?"

Kirby shrugged out of his coat and laid it over the back of an old, well-worn but comfortable looking couch. Olive stirred into movement when he reached to help her slip her coat off.

"For Bones?" He quirked an eyebrow at her. "Jill. I had written a few books by that time. Well, I'd written maybe a million and published a few. Jill's family had a dachshund when she was younger. And they called him Bones Malone."

"I love it."

"C'mon."

Caught up in Olive's genuine interest in and excitement for his work, for his and Jill's creation, Kirby reached for her hand, linked their fingers, and led her through the living area to the office at the back of the house. It crossed his mind that this was the first time he'd had a woman in the house since he'd lost Jill. He didn't think before he grabbed her hand, but he did notice that she didn't pull away from him.

Once in the office, he let go of her and stepped behind his desk. Olive wandered over to the far wall to study some of the framed illustrations of Bones, the longhaired dachshund detective who starred in his series and had made Kirby a household name in children's books.

"These are incredible," she said softly.

"Jill did those," he told her. "She did the first book. If you pay attention, you can see differences in my work."

"What does the M stand for?" She turned to look at him.

"Michael." He tapped the mouse on the desk and watched his screen come to life. "Which is my dad's name. So, I go by Kirby."

"And this is where you write?"

"Well. Mostly." He shrugged. "Where I work."

"Do you write them on the computer?"

"Sometimes. Jill had a studio upstairs where she painted. But it was...too hard." He sighed and met her eyes. "After she died, I had a hard time being in her studio, so I started doing a lot of the work down here."

"Do you do the illustrations in software?"

"I do." He nodded.

"Kirby, this is so cool." She tucked her hands in the pockets of her jeans, pulling Kirby's attention from her face and over her shoulders and the soft swell of her breasts under a baby blue sweater to her slender waist and tiny hips.

"C'mere." He nodded for her to come and stand by him behind the desk. The skip in her step pleased him. When she stood at his side, he could smell her perfume—something rich and heady that did things to his gut and his chest and even his neglected old friend, Dick. Did she feel this attraction, too? Or was she just excited about seeing the work in progress? If she was a reader, and she had said Lucia loved the books, then maybe she was just that excited about seeing the whole process.

He leaned over the desk and clicked into the current file —*The Poison Frog*— before stepping aside to let her look at the two illustrations currently finished.

"This is exciting!" She trilled a sweet little giggle. "I'm looking at the next *Bones Malone* book, in the writer's home office, standing right next to the writer."

"Are you a reader?"

"I love to read," she answered immediately. "I met Harlan Coben once. And I buy Luce all kinds of books. And to think she goes to school with your son."

"You read thrillers."

"I read everything." She straightened and looked up at him. "Have you written other stuff?"

"I had two books out before the series."

"And if I buy a book, will you sign it for me? Not for Luce. Me."

"I'll do you one better." He nodded and turned to pull a hardback copy of the first Bones Malone book from a stack on the credenza behind them. Olive watched as he opened it, grabbed for a marker from the middle drawer of the desk, and then scribbled his trademark autograph in the book.

Chapter Eight

OLIVE

"Thank you."

Olive took the book in both hands, like it was fragile, when he handed it to her. Eyes locked, they stood frozen that way —both holding onto the book—for a moment. For just a second, she wondered what it would be like to kiss him. Would she taste his coffee or the lingering sweetness of the bear claw on his lips?

A little bit breathless at the thought, Olive flicked her gaze over his face, lingering for a moment on his parted lips. And then she snapped out of the kissing fantasy and made herself look down at the book.

"This is great."

"Hang on."

When he let go of the book, she was oddly disappointed, as if they were connected there for a few seconds. He grabbed two more copies of the same book, set them gently on the desk, and signed both—the first to Lucia.

"What's the new baby's name?"

"Um." Olive cleared her throat, touched by his generosity. "Thomas."

He froze for a moment, still bent over the desk, and then turned his head to look at her with a knowing grin on his face.

"Lucia and Thomas."

Olive laughed softly. "Yes, my sister and brother-in-law are those obnoxious parents who name their children after their places of conception."

"Good thing they weren't in Detroit or Absarokee." He mumbled the words as he signed the second book to Thomas. Olive snorted and laughed out loud again. "We named Henry after Jill's grandpa. But Jill told her sister it was after the candy bar."

"Good one." Olive nodded her approval.

"Yeah, until her sister's then boyfriend said one day women might be calling out *oh Henry* when they're doing it. Kind of spoiled the whole thing for Jill."

"Not you?" she asked when he straightened and handed her the two books.

"Well, I mean, yeah, but you know." He shrugged and flashed a sheepish grin at her. "Go get 'em."

"No! Say it isn't so." Olive stepped back, the books now cradled in her arms like a baby.

"What?"

"You're not one of those *boys will be boys* kind of people, are you?"

"Of course I'm not." His eyes were wide and innocent when he looked at her. "But of course, I want Henry to find someone some day and fall in love and make a woman yell his name, too."

Olive tipped her head back and laughed.

"Guess it's just easier for a guy to think about his son eventually having sex than a mom, huh?"

"Well, imagine if you had a baby girl. You wouldn't like it either."

"I wouldn't. You're right. Henry has a crush on a second grader."

"So, he's into older women."

"Apparently, so." Kirby nodded with a big smile. "She's pretty cute."

"Well, so is he."

"He looks like Jill."

Olive thought about Kirby telling her that Jill wanted the house to be haunted, being disappointed when she'd seen or heard no ghosts here. She thought back to a few minutes ago when she'd wanted to kiss Kirby.

Something she hadn't wanted to do for a long time.

Maybe this house *was* haunted. Or *protected*, at least. By Jill's ghost. Her memory. Olive couldn't think about kissing a man in the home he'd shared with his wife. If he hadn't moved on, maybe that meant he was still in love with her.

"Do you wanna see the house?"

"I'd love to," she answered sincerely.

"Leave the books here," he suggested. When she put them on the desk, he reached for her hand again. Olive linked her fingers with his willingly and followed him into a clean, bright kitchen. Olive marveled at the white cabinets and the white counters, impressed with the clean lines and the natural light flooding the room from the windows on the southern wall.

"This is nice."

"Jill and I remodeled it when we first moved in."

"Did she cook?"

"Nope." Kirby shook his head with a laugh. "That was always my job."

"So, was the kitchen her vision or yours?"

"Hers," he answered simply. "She was always right, too."

Laughing softly, Olive moved slowly down the island counter and trailed her fingers over the granite top.

"How about you?"

"Do I cook?" She flicked her eyes back to him, a small smirk on her face. When he nodded, she shook her head. "Nope."

He led her into the living room where two books were side by side on a worn-looking coffee table. One was an adult historical fiction novel and the other was a picture book she'd read to Lucia just the other night.

"That's adorable." She hadn't meant to speak out loud. Kirby followed her gaze and his face lit up when he saw she was looking at the books.

"Have you read it?"

"I read it to Luce the other night, but I just meant both of the books there together."

Kirby tucked his hands in his pockets and tipped his head. "Henry and I have a pretty good routine. After school, he watches thirty minutes of TV and then either builds with Legos or spends time drawing, while I finish little things left from my workday. We fix dinner together—"

"Really?" Olive folded her arms over her chest and looked back at the books. The couch behind the coffee table looked cozy and inviting. There was a big screen TV on the wall, but somehow, Olive had almost completely overlooked it. One wall of the room was a bookcase with a few photos and knickknacks on it, but it was mostly filled with books. The TV seemed like an afterthought. "Henry cooks?"

"He likes to help." Kirby nodded. "He doesn't like to help with cleanup, but he gets to do that, too."

"I can relate to that."

"After dinner, we read. He reads to me. Spends a lot of time looking at illustrations. I read while he does that. And then he goes to bed."

"Nice."

"How about the studio?"

"I'd love to see the studio."

Used to his excitement now, to the way he grabbed for her hand to show her the way, Olive didn't even notice their fingers were linked until they were halfway up the stairs. They passed three closed doors on the way down the hall. Suddenly consumed with thoughts of which was Kirby's bedroom, Olive almost stopped walking to give herself a talking to. What had gotten into her? She'd quit going to clubs a few years back. Traded in the party days and the types of guys who were only out for a good time for quiet nights with friends and an occasional date with men who were supposed to interest her.

But didn't.

Not like this guy did. Single dad. Simple attire. Subaru SUV. And the seventies station playing in his car. She was wildly attracted to him, though she reminded herself with every step that she was out of line. She was in town to help Elaina and Mark. She wasn't here to meet someone—not for a fun little fling or anything else. Apparently, she needed to start getting out more if she was reading into the very nice, innocent way this guy was talking to her. He probably still felt guilty that she'd dropped her phone and keys into the mailbox.

Ridiculous. She didn't blame him even a tiny bit.

No, instead, she was picturing him in a cozy double bed with flannel pajama pants low on his hips and his hair wild and messy.

It was one thing to wonder what it would be like to kiss him.

Something else entirely to be imagining him in bed.

The studio was at the end of the hall. Kirby ushered her inside and watched her admire the room. A huge skylight provided incredible natural light. Olive wasn't an artist, but she understood the importance of good lighting for painters.

The walls in the spacious room were white—one wall covered with artwork. As she crossed the room to study the art, she realized some were paintings on canvas and some were sketched in ink. There were framed photographs mixed in the private gallery. Even a few pictures clearly done by Henry.

"This is the most incredible wall of art I've ever seen."

"Most of this is Jill's work."

"She was very talented."

"She was. And adventurous. She was always ready to try something new."

Olive glanced at him but looked away, struck by the look on his face as he studied the wall, too. Respect, maybe. Love. Sadness. All feelings anyone is entitled too when they lose the love of their life.

And yet, it made Olive feel a little sick and a little angry with herself for thinking inappropriate things about him just a few minutes ago.

Chapter Nine

KIRBY

"Henry has her talent." Kirby backed away from the wall of Jill's work and turned to look at Olive instead. After losing Jill, he couldn't come up here. He couldn't stand being in a room that was so filled with her presence. And then finally, one night he could. He'd spent hours working on his laptop up here. Writing. Writing other things—books he wasn't sure would ever see the light of day, letters to Jill. He'd done a bit of drawing up here, but the illustrations he did for his books were now all done with software, and he preferred using his desktop for that.

As much as he loved the room, as proud as he was of his deceased wife's work, he eventually stopped coming to the studio to feel close to Jill. Now that he stood here looking at another woman, he realized it had happened gradually, without him noticing.

Maybe because time had helped ease the knife of loss.

"I see some of his work here." Olive nodded. "He's a better artist than I am. I can't even draw stick people. And when I color, Lucia gives me heck for coloring out of the lines."

"Maybe that just means you're a free spirit." He shrugged when she glanced at him.

"This is great." She eyed the wall wistfully and finally turned back to him. "Thank you for hanging out with me. I'm fascinated by what you do here."

"But?" He tipped his head and quirked an eyebrow at her.

"I should get out of your way. Let you get something done."

Kirby didn't want her to leave. Or if she did, he wanted to go with her. But she was probably ready to get to the hospital. Get on with her life after a fun little stop for show and tell.

That thought beckoned him down the path of inappropriate thoughts again. *Show and tell.* The idea of this woman showing him things and telling him things she liked turned him on like nothing had in years.

"I'll take you to the hospital," he offered. "And come back to get you for the party."

"The party," she repeated with a laugh. "I still think she probably has the key to that damned mailbox in her desk, and she could have opened it to get my things."

"Maybe." He took a step toward her.

"On the other hand, if she had given me my stuff, I would have missed the chance to get to know you. And I'm glad I got that chance. This has been fun."

Was it his imagination, or was she leaning a little bit toward him? Just in case she was, Kirby took another step closer. He patted the back pockets of his jeans, relieved when she took the bait.

"What? Your phone?"

With a little shake of his head, he blew out a nervous sigh and arched his eyebrows. "Looking for the arrow that little dope must've hit me with."

The corners of her mouth tipped up the slightest bit, but her eyes lit up at his words.

"I like you, Olive Cullison."

He swept his gaze over her face, noticing the flush in her cheeks.

"Me too," she said with a breathless laugh. "What's up with that? Do you think *they* spiked our coffee?"

"No." He shook his head. "Because I was feeling this when we were in the classroom."

"I don't know what we do about this."

"Well, obviously, it's been a while since I've dated, but I think we could go out. Maybe for dinner. Or a movie. Or, we could do this."

She tipped her head up when he moved closer. He stood close enough to see the throb of her pulse in her throat, but he left a modest inch between their bodies. The scent of her rich perfume drove a strong need through him to possess her, but he didn't rush to take her. Instead, he lifted his hand and stroked his fingers over her face.

Thoughts on fire now, imagining the feel of the soft skin on her inner wrists, the backs of her knees, Kirby smoothed his thumb over her lips.

"Can I kiss you?"

"Yes."

Still cupping her face in his fingers, he leaned closer and kissed her. Just a soft press of his closed lips to hers. Again and again, each brush of his lips over hers stoking the fire inside him.

"I'm kind of rethinking my dislike for Cupid now." Her whisper was warm over his lips.

"I am, too." He drew back with a laugh and met her eyes. "I have to be honest with you, Olive. I'm trying to control myself, but I really want to do a lot of sexy things with you."

"Yeah?" She quirked an eyebrow at him. Kirby tried to swallow when she touched him, pressed her fingertips to his cheek and traced his cheekbone. "Which sexy things?"

"All of them."

She rewarded him with that trill of laughter he'd already come to love.

He kissed her again, swallowing the last of her laughter. Slow and easy, their parted lips met and stroked. He imagined sliding his tongue inside her mouth, but for the moment, just the feel of her wet lips on his made him high.

"I forgot how sexy kissing can be."

"Me too," she admitted.

Finally, they moved together, one last gentle, curious kiss before Kirby stroked her lips with his tongue. The tiny mewl in her throat sent his blood roaring through him, his cock thick and hard now. She kissed him back, her lips moving against his, her tongue rubbing and curling around his.

"Remember when you licked that marshmallow cream off your lip?"

Olive laughed and wrapped her arms around him.

"Mr. Owens, were you thinking dirty things about me even then?"

"Maybe."

He tugged her body close against his, hearing her catch her breath when she felt his erection between them.

"I haven't done this in a while," she whispered.

"Neither have I," he reminded her.

"I've never had a kindergarten hookup."

"Imagine the conversation hearts for what I wanna do to you."

"Can I still be your date to the party if I put out now?"

She watched him with a grin on her face, her eyes sparkling like stars.

"Are you sure? I know we just met, but this feels so good."

"Kirby Owens." She smoothed her hands over his shoulders and grabbed his shirt in her hands. "I want you to do dirty things to me."

Chapter Ten

OLIVE

This time when he took her hand to lead her from the room, Olive's belly fluttered with nerves. The good kind, though. The kind she hadn't felt in so long, it almost felt new. Anticipation. Excitement.

Kirby was right. This was crazy. Meeting him just hours ago in her niece's kindergarten classroom and now, she was following him down the hall and into his bedroom. It felt good. She was clearheaded, eyes wide open, and hungry for all the things they might do together in the bed they now stood beside.

Not like any times in the past, when she'd met someone and gone out with him once or twice and things had progressed to the next level just because it felt like that was what she was supposed to do. Olive wasn't proud to admit it, but there were times she'd slept with her dates just because it seemed like the thing to do. She'd stopped going out mostly because she was tired of meaningless casual sex with guys she could live without.

This was different.

Kirby Owens was different.

She might have just this one time with him, and maybe, she was going to be his bridge back into the dating scene and sex. They hadn't talked about things like that. Right now, it didn't matter to her. She liked him. A lot. He made her laugh, and the way he looked at her made her feel things other men's hands had never done.

"You're sure?"

His voice was gruff now. Olive had felt his erection pressed against her in the studio. Now she could see the lust and need in his eyes as he watched her, waiting again for her to say yes.

"I am."

He shot her a sheepish grin as he pulled his phone from his pocket and set it on the nightstand.

"In case your brother-in-law calls."

"God, I hope he doesn't call for a while," she said with a stutter of a laugh.

"Tell me to stop." He reached for her again and settled his hands on her hips. "If you change your mind."

Eyes locked with his, she nodded. He inched his fingers under the bottom of her sweater, and Olive shivered when the cool air kissed her bare skin. She fought the urge to tug the sweater over her head, suspecting that he wanted, needed, to do this part. To undress her.

And maybe, she needed this, too. The slow pace. The obvious pleasure he took from moving slowly, taking in every detail. Maybe Kirby Owens was going to give her something new. Because it struck her as he eased her sweater up further and his fingers caressed her bare belly, maybe Kirby was going to *make love* to her. And she wasn't sure *that* had ever happened before.

She lifted her arms when it was time, when he'd pushed her sweater up enough to reveal the navy lace covering her breasts. He eased it over her head and lowered it slowly, his hungry eyes roaming over her bare shoulders, the swell of her breasts over the lace.

"You're beautiful." His whisper was reverent.

"Your turn," she answered, taking his flannel shirt in her hands and pushing it up over his shoulders. Kirby shrugged out of the shirt and let it fall to the floor by her sweater. Again, Olive fought the need to rush, to shove his t-shirt out of the way and stroke his skin. Instead, she moved as he did, inching the shirt up little by little, her heart pounding —she felt it even in her fingertips—with each slice of skin she revealed.

He tugged the shirt off finally and watched her take in his broad shoulders, his well-defined chest, and the trail of hair that led down his belly beneath his jeans. Heart in her throat, she looked up at him in askance.

"Unless you want this to be over with really fast, the jeans need to stay on for a little bit."

She flashed him a quick smile before stroking her hands up over his chest and leaning closer to press her lips to his nipple.

"And maybe you shouldn't do that yet, either," he said with a laugh. "Maybe we should concentrate on you."

"Okay." She nodded as he bent his head to kiss her again. Olive felt a jolt of pure need deep in her belly, the flip-flop sensation shooting straight to her core. Kirby would find her panties wet when he got there. Suddenly, she couldn't wait for his response. Still with her mouth pressed to his, she reached behind her back and unhooked her bra.

"Beautiful," he said again as she drew away to slide the straps down her arms. Olive gasped softly when he ducked his head to nip at her nipples—both already painfully aroused. Overcome with lust, with the need for him to play there, to tease her with his tongue and soothe her with his lips, she moaned with pleasure when she felt his hands on the button of her jeans.

He kissed a trail down her belly, lowering himself in front of her, sliding her jeans over her hips and finally to the floor. Hands on his shoulders, she stepped out of them and watched him worship her again with hooded eyes.

"Can I—"

"Yes."

She didn't need to know what he was asking for; she wanted everything he would give her. And she was thrilled to give herself to him. With her head tipped down, she watched him scoop his hands up over the backs of her legs and sink his teeth gently into her inner thigh. His eyes were closed now as he kissed a line from her thigh up over her hip.

His hands cupped her bottom and then finally, he nipped again, a gentle love bite. She sighed with pleasure and impatience as he caught the tiny bit of lace on her hip in his teeth and slipped his fingers under the lace over her bottom. Within seconds, her panties were pooled at her feet, and she stood naked before him, eyes closed, and ready.

Expecting more, expecting to feel his mouth, his breath, between her legs, she whimpered softly in protest when he straightened in front of her, the warmth of his skin sliding over hers. Before she could say anything, before she could ask for more, he claimed her mouth in another long, wet kiss. Olive thrilled at the press of his chest to hers and smoothed her hands up over his arms and shoulders to cup the back of his head.

The drowning sensation, the gentle kisses peppered in with the long, demanding kisses, made her swoon on her feet. Hungry for the taste of his tongue, his lips, on hers, she held on tight and kissed him back.

"Ohmygod." She groaned out loud when he lifted her, wrapped her legs around his waist, and combed her fingers up through the back of his hair. "You're incredible, Kirby Owens."

He smiled against her lips as he turned and gently laid her on the bed.

"We're not even at the main event yet," he reminded her.

"I'm pretty sure it's gonna be just as incredible."

He drew back for a moment to stare into her eyes.

"It is," he agreed with a nod. "I think it will be."

With that, he dipped his head to rest his forehead against hers for just a second and then moved to catch her earlobe in his teeth. Olive wanted to touch him, to worship him, as he did her. But she was mesmerized by the way he moved over her, the kisses he gave her, the way he tasted her carefully, as if memorizing her skin and the way it felt on his tongue. When he closed his lips over her nipples—giving each of them careful attention—she arched her back to give him more and cupped his head to hold him there, letting her hand slide away only when he inched backwards and licked a trail to her belly button.

All thoughts gone, lost in the pleasure pain of his mouth between her legs, Olive writhed under him. He wasn't much of a talker, but she loved the quiet between them as he licked and suckled her sensitive skin. His hands stroked and smoothed and pressed her thighs and her belly and her bottom, and those touches spoke volumes—words she realized she had never heard or felt before.

When she came, hips off the bed, grabbing for more of him, he whispered to her. And oddly enough, even though this had never happened between them before, his awe-struck words were perfectly Kirby and perfectly thrilling.

"I got ya," he whispered as she thrashed in his bed, overwhelmed by the waves of pleasure he'd brought her, by the weight of his body between her legs, his warmth breath over her wet skin. "You are beautiful, Olive."

"I need you." She lifted her hands to rub her eyes, stunned by the tears on her cheeks. The intensity of her orgasm surprised her, but she still wanted, needed, more of him.

"I wish you could see what I see right now."

She laughed softly and lifted her head to look at him. "Yeah?"

"Well." He grinned. "I love what I'm looking at, but I mean the way your body reacted to me. The flush of color in your cheeks. The stars in your eyes."

"You're not looking at my eyes."

"Those beautiful breasts that I can't get enough of."

She laughed again. "Please?"

"Are you sure?" he asked. Before she could argue, tell him she was sure, he slipped his fingers inside her again and curled them just enough to make her arch her back again. "Do you want me to do this again?"

"I do," she whispered. And she did. Maybe later. After she felt his length stretch inside her. After they moved together and Kirby orgasmed, his body heavy over hers. Maybe later and again tomorrow and the day after. She couldn't say that now, though. That was a conversation for another time. "But I want to feel you inside me."

She watched boldly as he climbed easily over her and out of bed. He grabbed a box of condoms from the drawer of the nightstand, making her wonder for just a moment if she wasn't his rebound. His bridge. It didn't matter. Not in the moment.

Greedy for every inch of him, she fixed her eyes on his wiry forearms and down over his hands as he worked his jeans open and shoved them out of the way. His black briefs outlined perfect hips and a nice butt and his cock, big and ready for her.

Eyes locked with hers, he pushed the black material over his hips, and his cock sprung free as he kicked the briefs aside. Olive reached for the condoms, eyes on his hand as he fisted it and pumped his cock once, as if priming it to make love to her.

Her hands shook as she took a condom from the box and tore the wrapper open with her teeth. She didn't want to use it; she didn't want anything between them. She wouldn't get pregnant; she was on the pill. But it was too soon to be with him that way.

Maybe someday.

"Olive." He groaned as if in pain when she dipped her head and caught the tip of his cock in her lips. Before he could move, she flicked the head with her tongue and then drew away to roll the condom over him.

"I want to taste you," she told him.

"I need this first." He straddled her. "I need to be inside you so bad, I'm shaking."

He said it like a confession. Olive simply took his hands and linked their fingers.

"Me too."

He drove into her slowly, not so much with caution, but with awareness, making her ache and clench her walls around him, desperate to take him as deep as she could. When he was balls deep, he kissed her, their tongues mimicking the moves their bodies would make in a moment.

Finally, Kirby let go of her right hand, lifted her thigh, and began to move inside her. Olive felt the pressure, the stretch of her walls around him. His mouth on her neck. The arch of her back as she offered him her breasts again. The slide of his sticky skin overs. The pounding of her heart that surely he felt against his chest.

When she came this time, she urged him, the same whispered words, the same awe-struck feeling he'd expressed as he watched her come. Kirby moved faster, his hips rocking her harder and harder, until he tensed above her, and dropped his head to rest on her collarbone.

"Incredible," she whispered.

He tightened his fingers around hers and buried his face in her neck.

Chapter Eleven

KIRBY

Kirby hadn't spent a day in bed with a woman since his little boy was two and his wife was still living, and though he would always love Jill, lying like this, skin to skin with Olive Cullison after making love again and again, everything in his life in this moment was perfect. Watching her come undone at his hands and his mouth had been more than a turn-on. Kissing her so intimately, watching her shatter and hearing her moan his name as she writhed under him had been a gift.

Olive had given him her trust. She had given him her body to devour, but even more than that, she'd bared herself to him and shown him what passion and pleasure did to her. They'd only met a few hours earlier, but Kirby was beyond smitten with her. Not love. As giddy as he felt after hanging out with her, as content as he was after touching, kissing, every inch of her body and lying under her while she did the same to him, he knew it wasn't yet love.

He *could* love her. But Henry was too important to him to rush into any emotional ties. Kirby only hoped he would see her again, however that would work.

Even after making love, after exploring each other's bodies, Olive seemed content to lie in bed with him. Lazy and sluggish, nearly purring like a cat when he allowed his hands to explore again. Kissing him—she was greedy with his mouth, claiming his lips, his tongue, every few seconds.

When her brother-in-law finally called, they were tangled up together again, doing those same intimate things, and she had groaned in protest when Kirby leaned over her to snatch his phone from the nightstand.

"Hello?"

Lying under him, Olive sank her teeth into his shoulder when her brother-in-law asked to speak to her.

"Hey." She locked eyes with Kirby as she took the phone and greeted Mark. Kirby could hear both sides of the conversation, though the other end sounded a little tinny and distant.

"They're taking her back for surgery," Mark announced.

"Wait." Kirby moved when Olive's hand stilled on his back. "What? Why?"

"Baby's being stubborn," he answered. "They're doing a C-section."

"Why aren't you with her?"

"She wanted me to call you."

Olive cringed. Kirby pressed a quick kiss to her cheek and then slid away from her. She glanced at him with regret and sat up.

"Is she okay?"

"She's fine. Just ready to get this part over with."

Kirby stepped into his briefs and pulled his jeans on. Olive's soft laughter touched his heart. The ease with which she stood now, still gloriously nude in front of him, as she spoke to her brother-in-law stirred his lust again.

"Okay. I'll be there in a few minutes."

"Take your time."

"What time is it?" she wondered aloud. She looked around for a clock, Kirby assumed, and then met his eyes when she didn't see it. She offered him a small smile, looking a little shy for the first time since she'd blushed last in the studio.

"After noon."

Eyes still locked with Kirby's, she mouthed the word *WOW*.

"Need anything?" she asked her brother-in-law.

"We're good."

"Okay. See ya in a few."

Kirby held his breath when she ended the call and set his phone on the nightstand. Maybe he should have taken her to the hospital, rather than bringing her here to show her his work in progress. After all, she was in town to see her sister, to help out. But he hoped she didn't regret spending the morning in bed with him. As cliché as it sounded, Kirby hadn't enjoyed sex with a woman, *time* with a woman, like this since he was with Jill.

He wasn't naïve enough to think Olive felt the same way; that just because they'd spent hours pleasuring each other that she would automatically want to see him again. That maybe she felt something deeper than a physical attraction. But it would crush him if she confessed to regretting what they'd done.

"Hours, Kirby Owens." She stepped close to him with a whisper and pressed her bare breasts to his naked chest. "We just made love for hours."

That she chose to call it making love made him feel good.

"We did." He nodded.

"Who even does that?" She grinned.

He used to. With Jill. But maybe he shouldn't say that.

"You do," she answered herself. "Don't you? It's the kind of man you are."

"What do you mean?" He tipped his head and narrowed his eyes at her curiously.

"I've never been touched like you touched me," she said softly. "Like it mattered. Like you needed me to love the way you loved me."

"Of course it mattered." He shrugged. "Making love is about both of us. Not just what I want."

"Jill was a very wonderful, lucky woman." She stretched to her tiptoes to kiss him.

"She was," he agreed. "I think maybe you are, too."

"I think if I don't leave now, I'm going to crawl back into your bed and drag you with me."

Kirby linked his fingers behind her back and drew her into a deeper kiss. "Would that be so bad?"

She relaxed into his kiss, but within seconds, she laughed and pushed him gently back to give her space to dress.

"I wish I could stay," she told him.

"I get it." He picked her jeans up but hesitated. "You're welcome to use the shower if you want."

She laughed softly and nodded as she nibbled on her lip. "Probably a good idea."

"I'm full of them."

"Clearly."

"Help yourself. Towels are in the linen closet. I'll be downstairs, because if I stay up here waiting for you, I'll show you how I have no willpower. And I'll end up in the shower with you."

"Raincheck?"

"Absolutely, I'll take a raincheck on that." He grinned as he snatched his t-shirt from the floor. He tugged his shirt over his head and then watched her gather her clothing and cross the room to the master bathroom, eyes glued to her delectable bottom. Wishing he could indeed follow her into the shower.

Instead, he would go downstairs and fix her a light snack to take to the hospital.

And hope today was the beginning of something.

Chapter Twelve

OLIVE

"So, what you're saying is you spent the morning in bed with a stranger, practicing making babies while I was slaving away here trying to deliver this little monster baby?"

Olive lifted her gaze from the tiny blue bundle in her arms and met her sister's eyes.

"This is not a little monster baby," she corrected her. "He's adorable."

"You're right, he is." Elaina flashed her a dopey smile. "But the important part of what I just said was the first part."

"He didn't feel like a stranger," she said simply. "In fact, it feels like I've known him forever."

"Kirby Owens?" Elaina whispered when Mark pushed her door open to peek in. "Really?"

"Doing okay?" Mark looked from Elaina to Olive and back.

"We're having an important discussion," Elaina mumbled.

Olive snorted softly when Mark turned his deadpan face to her.

"You need some rest."

"I need the details," Elaina corrected him, eyes drooping even as she spoke.

"Details?"

Olive shook her head. "You don't wanna know."

He studied them for a few moments and finally nodded. "Olive, your friend is in the waiting room."

"He's not her friend," Elaina said with a little giggle. "She spent the morning boinkin' him, Mark—"

"Laine." Olive snorted and dropped her head back to stare at the ceiling.

"You did?" Mark stepped into the room with them and let the door close behind him. "Seriously? Do tell."

Olive rolled her eyes. "How about you take Thomas? Remember him? Your new baby." She stood and carefully placed the sleeping baby in Mark's arms. "And I'll say goodbye to my pain-in-the-butt sister and let her get some rest."

Totally focused on the baby now, Mark perched on the edge of the recliner. Olive leaned over to kiss Thomas's head and then turned to Elaina. Her sister was fighting sleep, clearly exhausted and needing the rest Mark suggested.

"I have a Valentine's party to go to." Olive wrapped her fingers around Elaina's bedrails.

"With smokin' hot Kirby Owens." A big grin spread over Elaina's face, though her eyes were now closed.

"Smokin' hot and generous to a fault," Olive whispered. Elaina opened her eyes for a second and tried to focus on Olive's face.

"'s good?"

"Love you." Olive kissed Elaina's cheek. "You guys make pretty babies."

"Henry Owens is pretty cute," Elaina mumbled.

"Goodbye Laine." Olive turned to her brother-in-law with a wink. "Want me to bring Lucia by later?"

"Call me. We'll see how Laine's feeling."

Olive nodded and crossed the room to leave.

"Liv," Elaina called as she pulled the door open. Olive looked over her shoulder and arched a brow. "He's a nice guy."

Olive blushed when Mark looked at her in askance.

"Party time," she reminded him and slipped out of her sister's room.

She found Kirby in the waiting room as Mark told her she would. What impressed her was the fact that he wasn't scrolling any social media apps on his phone. He wasn't looking at his phone at all. Nor was he watching TV. Slouched back in a semi-comfy-looking chair, right leg crossed over his left knee, he held an open magazine and for all appearances, seemed engrossed in something.

Olive watched him for a moment, a little stunned at herself and her behavior just hours before. She reminded herself it wasn't that far removed from meeting someone in a bar and spending the night with him, though she could count the number of times she'd done that on one hand.

She was more interested in the fall of his blond hair around his shirt collar than her scandalous behavior. Recalling the feel of the soft strands in her fingers, she fought the urge to go to him and comb her fingers through them now. He wasn't what society proclaimed as the perfect man—not physically anyway. She'd give Elaina that. Kirby Owens wasn't walking sex appeal, but he had *something*, didn't he? He'd charmed her hook, line, and sinker into bed with him, and now that Olive knew him so intimately, just watching him read turned her on.

"Oh, hey!" He turned to her with that big, warm smile—the one that had snagged her back in the kindergarten classroom—and stood. "Didn't see you there." He tossed the magazine down on the chair.

"What were you reading?" she asked as she approached him to stand closer.

"Hmm?" He arched his brows in askance and then glanced at the magazine. "Oh. A parenting article about building your kid's self-esteem."

"Kirby." Her hands moved without her brain's permission to rest on his shoulders. "I think you should be writing articles on parenting. Not reading them."

"You met my son for all of ten minutes this morning," he reminded her as he climbed to his feet. "He can be a hellion."

She laughed softly and shrugged. "Guess that's every kid, right?"

"Safe to say," he agreed. "How's the baby?"

"Adorable."

"Every kid," he repeated.

"No. My niece and nephew and Henry are exceptional," she said with a grin.

"And your sister?"

"Doped up."

"Can I kiss you?" He settled his hands on her hips and met her eyes.

"You have to ask?"

He shrugged and grinned sheepishly. "We're in public. Not sure how you feel about that."

She acknowledged his point with a nod. "I don't, either, but I think I'd like a kiss."

Olive noticed the flicker of happiness in his eyes when he leaned down to press his smile to hers.

"Are you ready to party, Olive Cullison?"

"I am so ready." She pecked his lips again before drawing away. "I'm dying for some fruit punch."

Kirby snatched their coats from the back of the loveseat by his chair. He helped her slip hers on before shrugging into his own.

"Henry said Libbie's mom was making cookies."

"Great. Donuts and cookies on my hips all in the same day."

Kirby slipped his arm around her shoulders as they headed out of the labor and delivery waiting room and down the hall. "I happen to love your hips. They taste even better than donuts and cookies."

Once outside, they linked fingers and jogged through the parking lot to his SUV. A light snow fell again as Kirby unlocked and opened her door for her.

"I know we agree on Cupid," he leaned into the open door as she buckled her seatbelt, "but where do you stand on Santa Claus?"

"He's awesome," she answered simply.

"Good woman." Kirby nodded, swung her door closed, and then hurried around to the driver's door. When he was settled and the SUV was running, he leaned over the console, cupped her chin in his hand, and kissed her.

"We're not gonna make it to the party if you keep at it," she whispered after long moments of a slow, intimate slide of their tongues together.

"Had to do that now, because I'm pretty sure kissing in kindergarten is not allowed."

Chapter Thirteen

KIRBY

Kirby found himself dishing up the fruit punch Olive had mentioned, only it was in the form of sticking straws in juice boxes rather than actually ladling punch from a bowl. He didn't mind; he volunteered in Henry's classroom on a semi-regular basis, and he enjoyed being around the kids. Today, though, was fun. And not just because of the things he and Olive had done this morning.

Watching her move around the room, talking to the kids about Cupid and Valentine's Day—she didn't bash Cupid to them—warmed him from the inside out. Olive Cullison was pretty; he'd clocked that two seconds after he bumped into her and knocked her phone and keys out of her hand and into the mailbox. But she lit up with the kindergartners —laughing and teasing and talking with them as if she didn't have a care in the world.

She'd done the same with him, he realized, as he watched her hand out Libbie's mom's cookies. Kirby knew for a fact that Libbie's mom worked and rarely made it into the classroom for anything, so it was especially sweet that Olive had taken the little girl by the hand and offered to help with cookie delivery.

Olive *had* lit up with him, too. Both in his bedroom and before, but in different ways, obviously. She was real, not some façade of what she thought women should be or even what she thought Kirby might want her to be. He supposed that said a lot for her self-esteem as well as her genuine trusting and nurturing personality.

He glanced at the giant Cupid cutout on the classroom door and gave himself a mental shake. Kirby didn't believe in the boogeyman or the tooth fairy any more than he did Cupid. (Santa Claus, however, was a different story. He was totally on board with Olive's assessment.) But how else did he explain the feelings whipping through him every moment spent around the woman he'd just met?

Sex.

Wasn't it just likely that he'd been without for just long enough that a warm, giving woman could come along and twist him up into a pretzel with those pretty eyes and the smile that lit up a room? With slender arms and legs and curves like those on back country roads? Lips that tasted sweeter than candy.

Sure. Kirby had to admit taking her to bed, making love to her, spending the morning in bed with her—all fantastic, and all things he prayed he would get to do again. He was a man, after all, and though he'd loved his wife dearly, he'd been alone for a couple of years. Of course his body was going to respond to a warm, willing woman as it had. Of course his *brain* was going to respond the same way.

But he wasn't *that* guy. *Never had been* one of those guys to treat women or sex as another notch on his bedpost. And even though he could admit that the sexual attraction was part of the draw to Olive Cullison, he felt like there was something more.

He considered checking his butt again to make sure there wasn't an arrow sticking out of it. Maybe it was in the center of his back, between his shoulder blades. Then again, there was no telltale arrow in Olive's back, and she seemed to feel the same as he did.

When the cookies were handed out and the kids each had a juice box to sip on, Mrs. Harlowe started the games. Kirby pulled a tiny chair next to Henry's spot at his table and sat. The kids got a kick out of it, but what he liked was the tickled laugh that came from Olive. She'd done the same, dragged a little chair to Lucia's table so she could sit with her niece. Kirby didn't think she looked as ridiculous as he did in the miniature chair.

They played Valentine bingo with conversation hearts. Olive gave him the side eye when Henry was the first to bingo. After five winners, clearing the cards each time, Mrs. Harlowe switched it up and they did an oversimplified word search. Kirby peeked at Olive when he saw the word list.

Kiss.

Luv.

Hug.

Mine.

XOXO.

More sappy Cupid stuff. But her little snicker when she caught him looking at her sent a wave of warmth over him.

Kind of weird to push this kind of thing at little kids. Silly games were one thing, but kisses and hugs and *be mine* and *love me* seemed more appropriate for older kids and adults. Kirby knew for a fact that Mrs. Harlowe focused the holiday on friendship and treating everyone equally, which was all well and good. But that didn't change the message in the conversation hearts or the Cupid cutouts around the room, did it?

Mr. Harlowe arrived with ten minutes left of class. He swooped in with a sack over the blue coat on his back. Dressed like a mailman, he hollered and waved at the kids, as if he were a wannabe Santa Claus. Kirby found himself searching out Olive's gaze again, wondering what she thought. She gave him an eye roll when their eyes met.

All Kirby could think was that it was a good thing Olive hadn't had an emergency where she needed her phone or keys. He understood Mrs. Harlowe's rule that they wouldn't open the mailbox for just anything, that no one could take back a Valentine once it was mailed. But she should have made an exception for an adult, for someone's parent or guardian, for Pete's sake.

Then again, if Olive had walked out of the classroom earlier with her phone and keys in hand, they might have shared a friendly smile and parted ways.

Even now, as Mr. Harlowe made a big deal of taking the key from the teacher, Kirby's stomach was in knots. Olive would get her phone and keys back. She had family here; she was busy with her sister and her niece and the new baby. She had a life in Normal—a job, friends, presumably an apartment or house.

Where did he fit in? *Did* he fit in? Or was today just a crazy hookup forever burned in his memory? He wouldn't blame her if that were the case. He liked her. A lot. He'd love to exchange numbers and get in touch now and again when she came to town to visit her family.

But he wanted more. He wanted to exchange numbers and call her now and then. To tell her about the St. Patrick's Day decorations Mrs. Harlowe would hang next month. He wanted Olive's thoughts on leprechauns and the pot of gold at the end of the rainbow. Text messages at odd times through the day—maybe a snapshot of a bear claw or a meme from social media, though to be honest, Kirby wasn't much for apps like that.

Mostly, he wanted her number and the knowledge that if he woke at three in the morning thinking about her, he could call her. He wanted to know he could hit her up for a sounding board when he was stuck on the current book. To share his other writing projects and passions and get her feedback. He hoped that she would think of him when she had something exciting to share or something heavy on her mind.

He wanted to know that on those occasions when Olive came in town to visit her family, she wanted to see him too.

Chapter Fourteen

OLIVE

Olive thought she might feel as excited to get her phone and keys back as the kindergartners did to get their Valentines. She didn't, though. In fact, she didn't even glance at her phone when Mr. Harlowe delivered it to her. Instead, she watched him wind his way through the classroom, dropping Valentines in each child's decorated bag. Most of the girls squealed with excitement over the pink, red, and white envelopes decorated with hearts and arrows as Mr. Harlowe dropped them in. The boys seemed more excited about the lollipops and fun-sized candy bars taped to some of the envelopes.

She flicked her gaze over to Henry's table to watch Kirby. The man still fascinated her, more so now. In the short time she'd known him, she'd seen him as a father, as a creator and businessman, a friend, and a lover. Watching him now as he watched Henry tug the wrapper off a sucker, Olive catalogued his features again. Sharp cheekbones, thick eyebrows, and bright blue eyes combined to make a pretty

83

face. She chuckled to herself; Kirby probably wouldn't want to be told he had a pretty face.

Now that she had her things, he could cut her loose. If this morning had all been just a whirlwind hookup, saying goodbye after this party could be it for them. Maybe she would bump into him from time to time when she was here visiting her family. But her life was in Normal, and Kirby had a life here. Olive had no way of knowing if she was special to him or if she was one of many women who had shared a passionate few hours with him.

Either way, she had no regrets. If they parted company today, and she saw him in the spring for a kindergarten talent show or a school picnic with the kids, she would be happy to consider him a friend and catch up with him as friends do.

But she wanted more. There was no way to know where things could go between them. After all, this was real life. Not some witty rom-com where Cupid really did exist, and Cupid really did shoot both her and Kirby in the butt with love arrows. But as she and Kirby and the other parents there as chaperones worked to help clean up the party and get the kids ready to go home, she found herself wanting to cross her fingers that there would at least be the possibility for more.

The thought made her laugh.

Crossing her fingers was as silly and superstitious as Cupid.

"Hundred bucks for your thoughts." Kirby spoke low, directly into her ear. His nearness, the feel of his warm breath on her ear made her shiver—thoughts of the way he'd kissed her there when he made love to her earlier twisting her belly into knots.

"A hundred?" she whispered and turned her head just enough to see him from the corner of her eye. "What does the tooth fairy pay in your house?"

"A buck," he answered, "but I put him in the same box as Cupid."

"Agreed."

"What're you laughing about?"

Mrs. Harlowe dismissed the students with parents in the classroom, so Olive and Kirby followed the crowd outside. Worried again that this might be the end of their crazy fun fling, she fought the urge to grab for his hand.

"Long story."

"Long story short." He nodded and shrugged.

"Well, after debunking the whole Cupid thing, I was about to cross my fingers that I would see you again."

Kirby met her eyes with a beautiful smile.

"And I realized that was the same kind of silly as Cupid."

"Clearly, we're both wrong about him, though." His voice was thoughtful as they walked to the parking lot. The snow had stopped before there was anything new to see on the ground. Just the same gray slush that had been driven through every day since the last big snow. The skies were gray, though, like any moment, it could snow again.

The parking lot was filling up with parents here to get their kids. The pickup line was in full swing. A row of buses waited in front of the school. It was anything but beautiful. But Olive decided the view, the whole day, ranked right up there with best day ever.

"Are we?"

"Can you do dinner with me tonight?"

She nibbled on her lip and stared at him silently for a moment. Lucia and Henry noticed they'd stopped walking and scurried back to stand at their sides.

"Aunt Olive, I wanna see baby Thomas."

Olive nodded and glanced at her niece. "We have to call Daddy and see if Mommy's awake."

"Then let's call her!" Lucia tugged on her arm.

"I'll have Lucia," Olive reminded Kirby.

"Bring her along. I bet she likes pizza as much as Henry."

"Luce, do you wanna go out for pizza with Henry and his dad tonight?" Olive asked without looking at her niece.

"Yes!" Lucia danced at her side. "But I want to see Thomas first."

"We'll call her."

"Gimme your number," Kirby said softly. "Unless you want me to call your brother-in-law and have him get ahold of you."

Olive snorted and reached for his phone. She added her name and number to his contacts quickly and then brushed her fingers over his hand when she handed it back to him.

"I will call."

"I hope you do."

"Let's plan on five thirty."

She nodded and drew back to look at him with surprise when he leaned close as if to kiss her. Instead, he brushed his cheek against hers and whispered to her.

"Pretend like I'm kissing you."

"Doesn't fit on a conversation heart."

He reached for Henry's hand as he stepped away from Olive. "Say hi to your brother-in-law. Seems like a nice guy."

For a moment, Olive simply watched Kirby and Henry walk away. Finally, she realized Lucia was tugging at her hand again.

"Is he your Balentime, Aunt Olive?"

"Why would you think that?" Olive linked her fingers through Luce's fingers and led her toward her own car.

"Because you're making soupy eyes at him."

"Soupy eyes?"

"That's what Mommy says to Daddy."

"Who does Daddy make soupy eyes at?"

"Me'n'mommy."

Olive looked at her niece to find the little girl watching her expectantly. "Yeah. I guess Mr. Owens is my Valentine this year, Luce."

Chapter Fifteen

FEBRUARY 14

K: Did you read *Bones Malone & The Blue Bird*?

O: Of course. Read it to Luce.

K: Too much the same if Bones Malone helps an injured squirrel gather acorns?

O: No.

O: And I think your text is just you fishing to talk to me.

K: We said we were going to text.

O: It's been an hour since we said goodnight after our date.

K: Sneaking to kiss you was fun. Made me feel like a teenager again.

O: 🤍

FEBRUARY 15

O: Mark put coffee in his cereal this morning.

K: On purpose?

O: No. Sleep-deprived.

K: Elaina and the baby ok?

O: She's good and the baby is precious.

O: Might steal him.

K: Move here and you can see him all the time. 😉

O: I see what you're doing there.

FEBRUARY 17

O: Do you draw?

K: ?

K: It's all on the computer now.

O: I know, but do you still draw?

K: Like ever?

O: Yep. Just random things.

K: Some.

FEBRUARY 17

K: Made meatloaf for dinner.

O: I feel the same about meatloaf as I do Cupid.

K: 😊 Not sure where we stand now on Cupid.

O: Eww.

K: But he brought us together.

O: 🤣

K: So you're saying you're not into meatloaf?

O: So much that, yes.

K: We can't be friends. 💀

O: But can we still be lovers?

K: Killin' me.

FEBRUARY 21

K: Happy President's Day

O: Let's not even go there.

K: 🤣

O: Luce lost a tooth last night.

K: And did the tooth fairy come?

O: She did. Luce got a dollar.

K: The tooth fairy is a guy.

O: What. Ever.

K: Serious. Tell me you saw *The Santa Clause 2 & 3*.

O: Fiction.

K: Favorite Christmas movie?

O: *Die Hard.*

K: I might be in love with you.

FEBRUARY 27

O: So nice to talk to you on the phone last night.

K: It was nice. I miss you.

O: Me too.

K: Let's make sure to do it more often.

O: k.

MARCH 1

O: Did I tell you Elaina thought she dreamt everything?

K: Everything?

O: Um.

K: ??

O: Never mind.

K: Nope. No recalls.

O: How's Henry?

K: I'll call you.

O: I told her about us. The day it happened. I told her I'd spent the morning in bed with you.

K: Oh. Wow.

O: That ok?

K: Yeah, unless she thinks I'm a perv now.

O: I'm the older sister, so no. And she thinks you're a stud.

K: But she thought it was a dream?

O: We were on the phone last night, and she got to laughing. Told me she dreamt I told that story.

K: Does that mean we're official?

O: We went out on a date. With witnesses.

K: Pint size witnesses that were more interested in debating *Spiderman* versus *My Little Pony*.

MARCH 7

O: Remember I told you my boss was looking to retire? Sell the business?

K: It was last night. My memory is bigger than an inch.

O: Everything about you is a good twelve inches, Kirb.

K: 😬

K: When did you say you were coming back for a visit?

O: You just said you remembered our conversation.

K: All the blood in my body just went straight south. Brain dead.

O: 🤭

K: So, did he sell?

O: Yep.

K: And? Is that good?

O: Dunno. Not impressed so far.

MARCH 10

K: Do you know the symptoms of strep throat?

O: Sore throat?

K: Henry's down with something.

O: Fever?

K: Yep. Taking him in.

O: Call me.

MARCH 15

O: Beware the Ides of March

K: Romeo & Juliet?

O: We can't be friends.

K: But we can still be lovers?

O: Have we made love?

K: Get your butt back here. Need you in my bed again.

O: Phone sex?

K: Better than sexting

O: Speaking from experience?

K: No. But if I'm gonna jack off while I talk to you, I want your voice in my ear.

O: I'll come over the weekend.

K: Good. Kind of feeling like I'm dying of thirst in a desert

O: You said it was way longer before we were together

K: Yeah, well, now I know what you taste like. Need you now.

MARCH 17

K: What about leprechauns?

O: Creepy little fuckers

K: Definitely in love with you.

O: But what about a pot of gold?

K: I'd run the other way.

O: You wouldn't take a single coin

K: No. My luck some leprechaun would curse me all the rest of my life

O: Rainbows?

K: Love them. Love to stand in the rain and look for them.

O: Might be in love with you.

Chapter Sixteen

OLIVE

"Why are you looking at me like that?" Olive asked her sister.

"How do you know I'm looking at you? You haven't looked up from Thomas since you got here five days ago."

"Been here two days," Olive corrected Elaina, "and who could look away from this sweet baby boy? I can feel your eyes burning a hole in the top of my head."

"So, you're still talking to him?"

"I am." Olive finally looked up to find Elaina curled in a ball in the corner of the sofa. "You look tired. Take a nap."

"Talk to me," Elaina argued. "Tell me about the sexy Mr. Owens."

"No."

"I don't mean those sexy things," Elaina said around a yawn. "Although, it's been a while, and some day I'd like to get back to that."

Olive offered her a smile when their eyes met.

"Just. Tell me about him."

"I think I'm in love with him."

Elaina stared at her for a moment and finally cocked her head to the side with a severe frown.

"What?"

Olive considered what she'd said and then whooshed out a big laugh, loud enough that Thomas stirred in her arms.

"If you wake that child, you are responsible for getting him back to sleep."

"Well, if he's hungry, the most I can do is buy him a burger, Laine." Olive shrugged. "I'm in love with Kirby Owens. Head over heels in love with him."

"*Kirby Owens.*"

"Why is that so hard to believe? He's an incredible man."

"I mean, he's nice, yeah." Elaina nodded. "He's just so...I don't know. Regular Joe?"

"And Mark is—what? Thor?"

"No." Elaina rested her head on the cushion behind her and rolled it back and forth. "No, I don't mean it that way, Liv. It's just...I've been seeing this guy every day since school started, and he's super nice. But he's—he's someone's *dad*. I guess I never thought of him that way."

"That's a good thing," Olive said firmly.

"But ya know what?" Elaina continued. "Mark is. To me. Mark is Thor. And Ryan Reynolds. And Mr. Universe and The Sexiest Man Alive."

Olive met her sister's eyes and nodded. "Yeah. It's like that."

"He's everything."

"We talk all the time," Olive told Elaina. "I mean, we talk on the phone almost every day. We text all the time. He texted me at two thirty in the morning once last week."

"I think that's sexting, and I don't need to know."

"He said he'd gone to sleep with his drapes open, and he woke up to see the stars in the sky. And it made him think of me."

"Cheese." Elaina rolled her eyes. "What? Like the stars in your eyes?"

"No. Just the fact that we've both always been under the same sky, the same stars."

"We all are."

"Stop killing the romance," Olive whined. "I really like him."

"I know." Elaina dropped her gaze to the baby when he started fussing.

"Why were you awake at two thirty in the morning?"

Olive groaned softly. "That's a whole other story."

"I'm all ears."

Olive laughed softly at her sister as her eyes drooped.

"What a captive audience."

"What's going on?" Elaina sat up straight. "Seriously."

"My job," Olive said quietly.

"Not liking the new ownership?"

"No. It's horrible." Olive shook her head. "They've let several people go. Seems like age discrimination."

"They can't do that. They have to have a reason."

"They fired one woman who missed a week of work because her little girl was in the hospital."

"Wow. That's heartless."

"I gave my notice."

"You did?"

"Yeah." Olive looked back at her sister. "So, now I'm starting over."

"Did you find something?"

"Not yet. I've had a few interviews, but nothing's come of them yet."

"Move here."

"What?" Olive blinked at her little sister.

"Move here."

"And do what?" She tipped her head curiously, the thought already taking root inside her.

"Work for me."

"Right." Olive nodded. "Because it always worked so well when we were kids, and I asked you to do something Mom told us we had to do."

"That's because you're not a good boss." Elaina waved Olive's protest away. "I am. And I need help."

"No, you don't. You're awesome on the job."

"I do. Because, hello? Newborn? Kindergartener? Business owner."

"I can't decorate—"

"You can," Elaina cut her off. "Your apartment in Normal is really fun, and you did that yourself."

"Laine."

"Work *with* me."

"Dad said you were the—"

"Dad was wrong." Elaina shrugged. "Look. You gave your notice. You need a job. I need help. You can decorate. You did a great job on Mom's sewing room when we were in high school. And also, I suck at keeping the books."

"Laine—"

"Seriously. Mark is helping me. I can't juggle everything anymore. And Mark is tired of the extra work."

"I'll just take the kids."

Elaina laughed. "And yes, if you lived here, you could take the kids sometimes."

"That's how you ended up with two kids," Olive reminded her with a laugh.

"Forget sex. I'm thinking eight hours of uninterrupted sleep."

"I don't know, Elaina—"

"Aaaannnndddd...."

Olive locked eyes with Elaina.

"You'd be able to see Mr. Owens as often as you wanted to."

She did like the sound of that. It was too soon to pack her things and show up on his porch and announce she was moving in. But she could find an apartment here. They could date. Olive loved the idea of spending more time with him and Henry, of having her sister and brother-in-law getting to know Kirby better.

Chapter Seventeen

KIRBY

Kirby dragged his attention from his computer screen when he heard Henry talking. Sure, his kid talked to himself sometimes and he talked to the TV sometimes, but he thought he'd heard another voice. Not a TV voice. Someone real.

A quick glance at the time stamp in the corner of his computer screen told him he'd been transfixed here a lot longer than he'd thought. Was Henry on the phone? Maybe Kirby's mom had called, and Henry had snatched the phone before Kirby even realized it rang. But that didn't explain the other voice Kirby heard.

He was on a roll, and he hated to shut his mind down when the writing was going well. But he'd made it a rule early on after losing Jill to never choose his work over his son. At least he was closing the file in the middle of a chapter, so he would know exactly where to jump in when he came back to his desk later. For now, he needed to see who Henry was talking to.

And then maybe they could go for a walk. Throw a frisbee at the park. It was a little breezy and chilly, but the fresh air would do them both good. Kirby stood, his mind already racing ahead to the rest of the afternoon and evening. He was already a bit hungry, so after a walk to the park, he would fix spaghetti—Henry's favorite. And after they read and Kirby tucked Henry in, he would call Olive.

He loved the now nightly calls with her. They'd quickly gone from calling once or twice a week to talking every evening. Kirby loved her voice—whether she was laughing at his crazy ramblings about pop culture or Henry or something he'd seen while grocery shopping or confiding to him about the flagging morale in her work environment.

And still, they kept a continuous streak of texts going, too. Fun stuff. An occasional rant. Memes. Kissy face emojis. Kirby hadn't seen that coming. A guy who didn't care for Cupid shouldn't use kissy face emojis, should he? He'd changed, though, hadn't he? He still didn't love the looks of Cupid, the idea of a fat baby boy interfering in things like love. But *something* had happened between himself and Olive on Valentine's Day.

He had finally told Olive about the middle school fantasy manuscript he was writing. Her enthusiasm for his new direction fueled him through the times of self-doubt. In fact, she'd proven insightful when he'd shared spots in the work where he was stuck, and they'd hashed out plot points well into the wee morning hours a time or two.

A little bit like he and Jill had done years before.

But different, too.

"Who are you talking to, Henry?" Kirby flipped the light off in the office and headed down the hall to the front of the house. "Is it Grandma?"

The first thing he noticed when he entered the living area was that the TV was on but muted. Henry didn't answer him, but when Kirby looked up, he found himself looking at the woman he'd been missing for the past month.

"Olive?"

"Hi."

"What're you—? Wow! I didn't know—" Kirby threw his hands up and cut loose with a helpless, but happy laugh. He hurried through the room toward the door where Henry and Olive were standing and scooped her up into a tight hug. Olive, gushing and laughing as unintelligibly as he was, threw her arms around his shoulders and held on.

"You," Kirby aimed a stern dad look at Henry, "are not supposed to answer the door unless I'm in the room with you."

Henry looked chagrined. It was a serious concern, one Kirby would hammer on again later. But right now, he was too happy to see Olive to lecture his son.

"Hope it's okay I'm here," she said softly as they drew apart.

"Totally okay." He kissed her cheek, mindful of the little boy watching them. "You didn't say when you would be here."

"Wasn't sure." She shrugged. "Were you working?"

"I was just knocking off, thinking it's a nice day to walk to the park."

"Can we?" Henry lifted up on his tiptoes, eyes wide with excitement. Probably the way Kirby had looked when he'd first seen Olive a moment ago.

"How are your frisbee skills?" Kirby eyed Olive suspiciously.

"Notoriously bad, but I'm game to go along and be the entertainment."

"Coat." Kirby glanced at Henry, but the boy had run from the room the instant he spoke. When they were alone, Kirby turned his full attention to Olive. "Hi."

"Hi."

As ravenous for her as he was, rather than devour her, he moved in with a patience foreign to him. He wanted to savor this—the first kiss since they'd had to say goodbye last month. He wanted to be in the moment as their lips brushed and parted, as their tongues dipped and danced together.

"Still got a thing for me?" she whispered.

Kirby settled his hands on her hips and tugged her in close. "I am over the moon for you, Olive Cullison."

Cupping his face in her hands, she smoothed her thumbs over his cheeks and pecked his lips again.

"We have things to talk about."

Kirby flinched and held his breath. "Most. Dreaded. Words. Ever." He tipped his head.

"All good things." She kissed him again. "Promise."

"Yeah?" He quirked an eyebrow at her.

"Yes."

"Dad, can we get a dog?" Henry bounded into the room and came to a stop nearly right on top of them—Kirby's arms still around Olive. "What're you doing?"

"I'm hugging Olive," Kirby answered. "And we'll see about the dog."

"*We'll see* means *no*," Henry informed Olive. "And you're only supposed to hug people you love."

Kirby pinched her butt when Olive snickered.

"Since when does *we'll see* mean *no*?"

"Like when I asked for a pony last year."

"That's different—"

"And when I asked if we could go to Disney last summer."

"Henry—"

"And when I asked for that Lego set last week."

"I think he's gotcha," Olive whispered. Kirby pinched her butt again, a thrill of warmth and love flooding him when she snorted and dropped her forehead to rest on his shoulder.

"So do you love her?" Henry asked when Kirby and Olive parted.

"Do I need a jacket?" Kirby eyed Olive in her fleece zip up.

"Probably not." She shook her head.

"Then why do I have to wear a coat?" Henry whined.

"'Cause I'm the dad, and I said so."

Henry rolled his eyes. Kirby nodded toward the hall. "Let's go out the back, so we can grab a frisbee."

Thankfully, Henry grabbed Olive's hand and led her down the hall, chattering about the picture he drew earlier of Zuma from *Paw Patrol*. Kirby would rather not discuss how he felt about Olive with Henry until he told *her* how he felt. Quickly, he locked the front door, found the remote to turn the TV off, and hurried down the hall after them.

Chapter Eighteen

OLIVE

Henry ran ahead of them as she and Kirby walked hand in hand down the sidewalk. Part of her wondered what Kirby was thinking regarding the two of them as a couple and Henry. He hadn't answered Henry at the house when he asked if Kirby loved her. Olive wanted to know if Kirby loved her, but she wanted him to say it to her. Not Henry.

She felt a little guilty for not telling Kirby how she felt about him before the words had come gushing out of her mouth at Elaina's last night. But she had only made the realization as she and Elaina talked. Kirby would understand that. She had considered going to him last night, after the kids were down and Elaina and Mark were resting.

But a little slice of her brain had made her wait. Everything she'd already shared with Kirby had been a rush—a good rush, the thrilling feel of the free fall from the high dive. Olive decided to give her heart the night to think and feel about Kirby, to see what the morning brought.

The morning hadn't changed her mind.

No matter what came of her and Kirby, Elaina had all but talked Olive into moving back and working *with* her. Elaina had stressed that point several times through the evening, including when she unceremoniously brought the whole matter up to Mark over dinner. And no matter what kind of feelings she and Kirby might be flirting with at the moment, she most definitely hoped they would see each other more if she moved back.

But morning hadn't changed her mind or heart about loving him. She had waited to be sure so she wouldn't rush at him and declare her love and push things too fast—she had to laugh any time she thought that, after the way they got together—and end up hurting someone.

She loved him. *No*. Olive Cullison was *in love* with Kirby Owens. And ready to tell him so.

"Can't believe you didn't get him a pony last year," she said now as they crossed the street and made a right turn toward the park.

"How would I fit a pony under the tree?"

She rolled her eyes. "I thought only girls wanted ponies."

"Well, that's sexist." Kirby shook his head.

"What about the Lego set?"

"I'll get it for him eventually," he answered. Olive watched him as they walked. Kirby kept his eyes on Henry, glancing at her now and then. "Honestly, I would have bought it that day. I think all the building things are good for him."

"But?"

"He was tired, and he was having a bad day."

"Ah." She nodded. "Got it. Has he ever told you he hates you?"

"No." Kirby cringed. "Not ready for that."

"Luce has told Elaina that a time or two."

"I think they learn that stuff at school."

"What about the dog?"

Kirby turned his head and grinned. "When am I gonna get you alone? I am dying to kiss you all over."

"Don't change the subject on me."

"I don't know. Dogs are a big responsibility."

Olive watched Henry run at the jungle gym as they entered the park. He dropped the frisbee as he climbed up the red rungs to the slide.

"I gave my notice."

"Good." He nodded. They'd discussed her job, the new owners and management over the phone. Each time, Olive had been more and more distressed and anxious over the situation. "Okay, so this is what we need to talk about?"

She started to agree but caught herself. This was one thing she wanted to talk to him about, yes. But it wasn't the most important thing on her list, not by a long shot.

"Sort of?" She shrugged.

"Daddy! Watch me!" Henry yelled from the top of the slide.

"Watchin' ya, buddy!"

Both of them stopped at the swing set and dropped into swings side by side.

"Sort of?" Kirby prompted her.

Olive hesitated. Did she want to do this here? She had imagined something more private, intimate. Who knew when they would get to that, though, with Henry in the house? Olive wanted to be with Kirby as badly as he wanted her, but she would play by the house rules as far as Kirby's son was concerned.

Then again, where better to tell this incredible man that she was in love with him than a city park on a pretty spring evening with his son enjoying the jungle gym. After all, it was Kirby's big heart with his son, his compassion and his tenderness with Henry, that had drawn her to him in the first place.

"I told Elaina this first," she admitted. "And I feel bad about that."

"You told Elaina that we had sex before the sheets were cold, too," he said with a shrug. "So, there's that."

Eyes locked, they shared a quiet laugh.

"I love you."

He didn't answer her immediately. But he didn't have to. The look in his eyes, on his face, said everything. Olive held her breath, anyway, hoping she hadn't spoken too soon. Finally, Kirby dug his feet into the wood chips below them and pushed his swing close to hers.

"I love you, too."

He grabbed the chains of her swing, leaned around them, and kissed her. Soft and sweet but still possessive.

"Gross!" Henry yelled from the playground equipment.

Kirby and Olive drew apart and turned their gazes to the little boy.

"What about Henry?" she asked quietly. "Will he be okay with this?"

"He doesn't even remember Jill, if that's what you're asking."

"But will he be okay with sharing you? With me?"

"I think so." Kirby looked back at her.

"I'm um…" She took a deep breath. "I'm thinking of moving back here. Elaina asked me to work with her."

"You're—?"

The grin on Kirby's face lit up the park like sunshine.

"If you think you want me around more."

"I want you around more," he told her immediately.

"I thought maybe we could do the things."

"You don't know how badly I want to do all the things."

Olive snorted and rolled her eyes when Kirby waggled his eyebrows.

"Dinners. Movies. Dancing."

"You want to date me." The sly grin on his face amused her.

"I want you to court me."

"Court you," he repeated.

"I think that's the perfect word for it. For us." She nodded. "You are the most chivalrous, generous man I've ever met."

"I can be dirty," he reminded her. "Or have you forgotten?"

"Even when you're dirty, you're generous, Kirby Owens."

"Can we throw the frisbee now?"

Henry had appeared in front of them like magic. Olive sneaked a peek at Kirby, surprised when the boy took her hand instead of his dad's.

"Yes!" She climbed from the swing. "But I'm not a very good frisbee thrower."

"Me neither," Henry told her.

"This could be trouble." She heard Kirby mumble behind them.

Chapter Nineteen

KIRBY

Kirby whistled to himself as he skipped up the steps to the porch of Olive's rental house. He had pitched in last weekend and helped her move. He and Mark had done the heavy lifting, though Olive hadn't shied away from hard work. Kirby knew she was trying to keep Elaina from overdoing it after the C-section.

The house was a white vinyl-sided bungalow. It suited her. Just over a thousand square feet, two bedrooms, and a kitchen he couldn't wait to christen. Or cook in, for that matter.

He hadn't been back since she'd settled in. They'd talked every day the last week, but Kirby wanted to give her a little space and time in the house and working with Elaina. While the house itself was in good repair, the landscaping left a little to be desired. Olive was champing at the bit to dig in—literally—and plant some flowers.

Speaking of flowers, he passed the bouquet of yellow roses to his left hand and rapped the knuckles of his other hand on the door. If Olive Cullison wanted to be courted, he was up for the challenge. In fact, he would go above and beyond and rock her world.

"Hey." She opened the door with that smile that rocked his. Dressed in yoga pants and a loose-fitting tee, she obviously wasn't expecting him. "Hi. Oh."

"These are for you." He pressed the bouquet into her hands and leaned in to kiss her cheek.

"Kirby, they're beautiful."

"Made me think of you," he said simply. True and not—yes, he had seen the roses in a florist's ad for Easter and thought of her. But, no, he didn't need a special day or thing to bring Olive to mind.

"Where's Henry?" She stood on her tiptoes to see over his shoulder.

"He's with a babysitter," Kirby told her.

"Oh." She blinked and stepped backwards. "And you're here. At my house. Where we're alone."

"Indeed." He grinned. "We have dinner reservations in an hour."

"What?" She stared at him with wide eyes over the roses. "I thought we would..."

Kirby loved the little shrug and smirk, and he loved where her mind had gone and what she wanted. But first, he would romance her. And then he would make love to her.

"Dinner," he repeated. "I got a lead on a good wine we can try, too."

"Dinner." She nodded but still didn't move.

"Do you wanna go as you are?" He tipped his head and let his eyes roam down over her hips and shapely legs. "I'm good with it, but—"

"You look fantastic," she interrupted him.

Kirby cast a self-conscious look at his flat front khakis and blue button-down shirt.

"Give me forty-five minutes." She pressed up on her tiptoes again to kiss him and then whirled away to get ready. Kirby laughed when she rushed back at him and handed him the roses. "Vases in the cabinet over the fridge."

"I'll take care of it," he promised.

She hurried off again toward her bedroom but paused at the door.

"Kirb?"

"Hmm?"

"Where do you stand on the Easter Bunny?"

"Somewhere between the tooth fairy and Cupid."

"Why are they all male?"

"You argued that the tooth fairy is female."

"You say she's not."

Kirby leaned back on the door and crossed his legs.

"Clock's tickin'." He shrugged. "I will drag you out of the shower and take you to dinner naked."

"You wouldn't do that!"

"I'd knock first," he said with a wink, "but I would do that."

They stood in place for a moment—Kirby at the front door and Olive at her bedroom, eyes locked, smiling like lovesick fools.

"The Cupid thing," she said with a shake of her head.

"It's gonna make a great story for the kids and grandkids someday, don't you think?"

THE END

IF YOU ENJOYED READING KIRBY & Olive's story, please consider leaving a review on your favorite bookish site!

Sneak Peek at Intoxicate Me

Chapter 1

The quirky little blonde wiggled her body against his again. The bar was hopping, and the dance floor was packed, but he'd seen it crazier. She had room to dance; she was coming onto him. Malachi wasn't big on dancing; his buddies had talked him into this. So Roman was getting married. What the hell happened to doing the bachelor party at a strip club? Or throwing a bachelor party at someone's house or a hotel and bringing the strippers in?

What the hell had happened to the *bachelor party*? What the hell happened to his buddy? Pussy-whipped, that's what.

Aria doesn't want to do the traditional bachelor and bachelorette parties. Aria wants to do a couples' night out. Aria wants....

Sure, Mal liked Aria okay, but he wasn't sure he liked the way she was changing his best friend. Hell, they were too young to do this commitment stuff, weren't they? They'd only been out of school for a year or two. Okay, three. And

Roman and Aria had been seeing each other for two of those three years.

Still. Malachi Murphy wasn't about to get caught up in a committed relationship. And he wasn't into nightclubs. Hell, he was a good ole boy. He liked bonfires and Luke Coombs and longnecks. Country girls with long legs.

But maybe this little blonde would do for tonight.

"She's into you, Mal!" Aria leaned close to him and yelled so he would hear her over the music. Some kind of remix of an old Elton John song. Roman arched his eyebrows as if to say why not? Mal turned on the dance floor, barely moving his hips to the beat. The blonde flashed a smile—maybe a bit more manic than sexy—but he had to admit she had some moves. Those little hips gyrated perfectly to the beat of the music.

Hell, why not? Damned near all of his buddies were dancing with someone. Some of them, like Roman, were caught up in relationships. Some of them just feeling the beat, the alcohol mostly, and the hot curves pressing up against them.

The blonde barely came up to his shoulder. Even in the heeled sandals. Mal took advantage of her spin and eyed her from head to toe. Her honey blond curls were piled in a messy knot at the back of her head. The lacey red tank she wore left her tan, toned arms exposed. Mal had a thing for collar bones and long, elegant necks. The tank stopped at the faded skinny jeans painted on her little hips, still swinging to the beat. The denim molded her lean thighs and calves and led him right down to the red fuck-me heels.

His dick jumped to attention. Maybe he wasn't big on clubs and dancing, but that didn't mean he couldn't do it. And damned if her moves weren't sexy as fuck. He could play along. See where it led. The idea of stripping those jeans off her made his mouth dry. He reached for her hand when she faced him again. She flashed another smile. This one was smaller, less certain. Fuck if that didn't turn him on even more.

Thank fuck his sisters had taught them all how to dance. Maybe not the part about grinding middle to middle, but Breena and Sarah had taught him and his brothers how to move on a dance floor. Didn't hurt that they were athletic and well-built. And apparently, they all had rhythm.

Behind him, he heard Roman cut loose with a loud catcall. He knew his buddy was referring to the way he was now moving with the blonde. Fuck it. He didn't care. The rest of the guys were having a good time; he was going to enjoy himself, too.

If the blonde said goodnight when the dance was over, so be it. His daddy had taught them all to respect women. He'd also taught them all to appreciate the love and loving of a good woman. Mal's parents were still so in love and so handsy, he and his siblings were often telling them to get a room.

Maybe it was the beer, but the girl could sing, too. Every now and then he heard her butterscotch voice sing out a lyric. Decided he liked the sound of it. Wouldn't mind hearing that voice calling out some four-letter words, his name, God's name—*whatever*—while they did some horizontal dancing. Until then, he threw himself into the groove, circling the blonde, standing close and swaying to the beat, shaking and stepping in time to the music.

Hell, maybe now he would be a big Elton John fan. He didn't dislike him, but his music usually made him think of rainy days. Nothing fun and sexy like this. Mal was still dry; he'd finished his last beer a while ago, and he was in pretty desperate need for another. But damned if he was going to leave this hot number out here to latch onto someone else.

The music changed from the electronic dance song to the slow number all the girls went nuts for in the movie. The one with Lady Gaga and Bradley Cooper. Hell, Mal's mom and sisters could mop the floor with their tears over that movie, and they weren't a whole lot more put together just hearing the song. Mal wasn't into it. Least now he could go grab a beer. Go tell the DJ thanks for the cockblock music.

The blonde had other plans. Before he could take a step— the crowd on the dance floor here had doubled when he wasn't paying attention—she slid her hands up over his shoulders and looped her arms around his neck. When the Lady Gaga part started, the blonde started singing along. Mal was mesmerized by her mouth. The idea of those shiny ruby red lips leaving lipstick marks on his dick made his chest ache.

Fuck. He was sweating.

He and his siblings had gone to Catholic schools, being the good Irish family they were. Mal had his doubts about his current dance partner. She was pressed to him like a postage stamp; no room for Jesus or even the Holy Spirit between them. His older brothers had told him bad girls were more fun. Not that he hadn't learned that for himself by now.

"Sing with me."

Mal laughed at her suggestion. He only knew what she'd said because he was watching her mouth so closely, wondering what she'd been drinking. What her tongue would taste like. What the rest of her would taste like.

"Not a good idea." He shook his head.

She grinned, still singing, and loosened her grip on his neck. His dick throbbed again as she smoothed her fingers over his lips. No way she didn't feel his hard-on poking the fuck out of her middle. She met his eyes now as she sang.

Maybe she was a witch, because before Mal knew what was happening, he was singing with her. He didn't even realize he knew the words. But then again, how could he not when his mom had played the song on repeat for a good 47 days after the movie came out?

About the Author

Tracy Broemmer is the author of several contemporary romance novels including The Mississippi Queen Trilogy, The Jane Thing, and Shameless Santa. Tracy also writes women's fiction and is the author of the Williams Legacy series as well as several stand-alone titles.

Tracy's books have been called gripping, emotional, and timely, and readers describe her characters as real and relatable.

Tracy lives in Midwestern Illinois with her husband of 29 years. Visit her on the web and sign up for her newsletter at www.broemmerbooks.com

Also by Tracy Broemmer

Women's Fiction Novels:

Luther's Cross (10th Anniversary Edition)

Fairytale (Writing as Therese Kinkaide)

Just Like Them

Small Hours

Picket Fences

Two Story Home

Green-Eyed Girl

Say Everything

Come Home for Christmas

Sketching Litchfield Lake

Ever, Again

Safe as Houses

Damsel

The Valentine Suite

Women's Fiction Series in Order

Lorelei Bluffs

Every Little Thing

Two A.M.

Blind

Leaving July

Hesitation Marks

Four Letter Words

See Kate

Loved You More

A Lorelei Ending

I Do

The Williams Legacy

Truth Is

Other People's Ugly

Omissions

Women's Fiction Short Stories

India Falls

Luther's Cross: 87,600

The Candy Cane Tree of Willow Lane

Delays

Same Time Next Year

Contemporary Romance Novels

Destiny's Calling: Your Future is Waiting

Wedding Day Shenanigans

Holiday Fling

The Kiss Off

Something Like Love

Plus One

End in Flames

Contemporary Romance Series In Order

The Mississippi Queen Trilogy

Love, Nashville

Forever, Duncan

Always, Jess

Truly, Dante (A Short Story)

The H Books

Gettin' Hitched

Hookin' Up'

Holdin' On (A Novella)

Timberton Hounds (Novellas)

Priceless Memory (A Short Story)

Endless Summer

Homeless Holiday

Restless Hearts (Currently included in Fall Into Love, an anthology by Fluffy Fox Publishing)

515 Whiskey

Intoxicate Me (A Novella)

Taste Me

Kissing Springs Trio

Shameless Santa

Sunshine & Soulmates

Bourbon & Bedposts

Lockland Distilling: Keys to Love Trilogy & Kissing Springs World

Leaving You (A Short Story)

Seducing You (A Novella)

Kissing You (A Novella—currently included in the Let's Get Naughty, Volume 2)

Shared World Novels

Hold Onto the Stars (Blue Collar Romance Series, Book #5)

The Jane Thing (Meet Cute Book Club Series, Book #2)

Shameless Santa (Welcome to Kissing Springs, Book #7)

Doctor Divine (Doctors of Eastport, Season 2)

Sunshine & Soulmates (Welcome to Kissing Springs, Book #

Bourbon & Bedposts (Welcome to Kissing Springs, Book #

Moonlight in Montreal (The Vagabond Series)

Beach Daze (Flamingo Island)

Christmas & Other Inconveniences (Betting on Christmas Collection)

Love in Motion Duet (Novellas)

Feels on Wheels

Rings on Wings

The Wine Tasting Series (Short Romantic Stories)

Perfect Pictures (Traminette)

Coming Home (Edelweiss)

Save Me Every Dance (Rosé)

Marry Me (Shiraz)

Birthday Wishes (Muscat)

Dad Jeans (Vignoles)

Contemporary Romance Novellas

Boone's Girl

Today, Again

Indian Summer

Dear Jaclyn Perris

Mistletoe Mishaps

Deadman's Hollow

French Stuff

Holdin' On

Toasted

End in Flames

Endless Summer

Homeless Holiday

Feels on Wheels

Rings on Wings

Intoxicate Me

Contemporary Romance Short Stories

Truest Love (Currently included in Show of Dreams anthology)

Swipe for Fangs (Currently included in the anthology Welcome to Whynot)

Mrs. Bennett

Peppermint Lane

The Principles of Accounting

Strawberry Wine

Love Letter

Sambuca Santa

Truly Dante

Leaving You

Priceless Memory

Perfect Pictures (Traminette)

Coming Home (Edelweiss)

Save Me Every Dance (Rosé)

Marry Me (Shiraz)

Birthday Wishes (Muscat)

Dad Jeans (Vignoles)

Other Novellas

The Devy Man, A Horror Novella

The Keeper's Heart, A Horror Novella

Anthologies

Just Coffee — French Stuff (2020)

Snowed Inn, Vol. 1 — Holdin' On (2020)

Aced, Back to School — Boone's Girl (2021)

Snowed Inn, Vol. 2 — Delays (2021)

Sweet Treats — Peppermint Lane (2021)

Sweet Sprinkles — Same Time Next Year (2022)

Rescue Me — End in Flames (2022)